TIME OUT!

The year 2490 is suddenly a nerve-wracking time to be alive. An escape has been found from a crushingly overpopulated and overregulated world: escape into the past.

The society is terror-stricken: any one of the time hoppers, by the slightest rearrangement of the time into which they hop, might destroy contemporary reality and—among other possibilities—cause anybody to cease to exist!

THE TIME HOPPERS

Robert Silverberg

AN AVON BOOK

AVON BOOKS
A division of
The Hearst Corporation
959 Eighth Avenue
New York, New York 10019

First Avon Printing, October, 1968

Cover illustration by Don Punchatz

Printed in the U.S.A.

for Michael Moorcock

One can conceive of Heaven having a Telephone Directory, but it would. have to be gigantic, for it would include the Proper Name and address of every electron in the universe. But Hell could not have one, for in Hell, as in prison and the army, its inhabitants are identified not by name but by number. They do not *have* numbers, they *are* numbers.

—W. H. Auden, *Infernal Science*

That Time should be a length travelled over is, all said and done, a rather elaborate conception; yet that this is the way we do habitually think of Time is agreed to by everyone, both educated and—which is much more curious—uneducated. . . . How did we arrive at this remarkable piece of knowledge?

—J. W. Dunne, *An Experiment with Time*

one

There was a beauty in the crowded world, so they said. The crystalline city towers in serried ranks assembled, the patterned rhythms of a surging mob at a quickboat ramp, the dance of sunlight on a million iridescent tunics in one of the great plazas—in such things, the esthetes said, was the abode of beauty.

Quellen was no esthete. He was a minor bureaucrat, a humble civil servant of decent intelligence and normal proclivities. He looked at the world as it presented itself in A.D. 2490, and found it hellish. Quellen was unable to perform the intricate inner dance by which hideous overcrowding could be written off as modern beauty. He hated it. If he had been Class One or even Class Two, Quellen might have been in a better position to appreciate the new esthetics, because he would not have been required to live right in the middle of them. But Quellen was Class Seven. The world does not look quite the same to a man in Class Seven as it does to a man in ClassTwo.

And yet, all things considered, Quellen was not too badly off. He had his comforts. Illegal comforts, true, obtained by bribery and cajolery. Strictly speaking, what Quellen had done was shameful, for he had taken possession of that to which he was not entitled. He had pocketed a private corner of the world, just as though he were a member of the High Government—that is to say, Class One or Class Two. Since Quellen had none of the responsibilities of the High Government, he deserved none of the privileges.

He had taken those privileges though. It was wrong, criminal, a betrayal of integrity. But a man is entitled to a

9

fatal flaw of character somewhere. Like everyone else, Quellen had begun with high dreams of rectitude. Like nearly everyone else, he had learned to abandon them.

Pong.

That was the warning bell. Someone wanted him, back in the miserable warrens of Appalachia. Quellen left the bell alone. He was in a tranquil mood, and he didn't care to puncture it simply to answer the bell.

Pong. Pong. Pong.

It was not an insistent sound, merely an obtrusive one, low and mellow, the sound of a bronze dish struck with a felt-covered hammer. Quellen, ignoring the sound, continued to rock uneasily back and forth in his pneumochair, watching the sleepy crocodiles paddling gently through the murky waters of the stream that ran below his porch. *Pong. Pong.* After a while the bell stopped ringing. He sat there, joyously passive, sensing about him the warm smell of green growing things and the buzzing insect noises in the air.

That was the only part of Eden that Quellen did not like, the constant hum of the ugly insects that whizzed through the calm, muggy air. In a way they represented an invasion; they were symbols to him of the life he had led before moving up to Class Seven. The noise in the air then had been the steady buzz of people, people swarming around in a vast hive of a city, and Quellen detested that. There were no real insects in Appalachia, of course. Merely that symbolic buzz.

He stood and walked to the rail, looking out over the water. He was a man just short of middle years and just above middle height, leaner than he once had been, with unruly brown hair, a wide, sweat-flecked forehead, and mild eyes of a shade not quite green and not quite blue. His lips were thin and tautly compressed, giving him a look of determination instantly belied by a less than affirmative chin.

Idly he flipped a stone into the water. "Get it!" he called, as two crocs glided noiselessly toward the disturbance in hopes of nabbing a fat gobbet of meat. But the stone sank, sending up black bubbles, and the crocs bumped their pointed noses lightly together and drifted apart. Quellen smiled.

It was a good life here at the heart of darkness, here in tropical Africa. Insects and all, black mud and all, humid solitude and all. Even the fear of discovery was supportable.

Quellen rehearsed the catalog of his blessings. *Marok,* he thought? *No Marok here. No Koll, no Spanner, no Brogg, no Leeward. None of them. But especially no Marok. I miss him the least.*

What a relief it was to be able to stay out here and not suffer their buzzing voices, not shudder when they burst into his office! Of course, it was wanton and immoral of him to set up shop as an *übermensch* this way, a modern Raskolnikov transcending all laws. Quellen admitted that. Yet, he often told himself, life's journey was a trip he'd take only once, and at the end what would matter but that he had traveled First Class part of the way?

This was the only freedom, out here.

And being far from Marok, the hated roommate, was best of all. No more to worry over his piles of undone dishes, his heaps of books scattered all over the tiny room they shared, his dry, deep voice endlessly talking on the visiphone when Quellen was trying to concentrate.

No. No Marok here.

But yet, Quellen thought sadly, yet, the peace he had anticipated when he built his new home had somehow not materialized. That was the way of the world: satisfaction draining off into nowhere at the moment of attainment. For years he had waited with remarkable patience for the day he reached Class Seven and was entitled to live alone. That day had come; but it had not been enough. So he had purloined Africa for himself. And now that he had encompassed even that, life was simply one uneasy fear after another.

Restlessly, he shied another stone into the water.

Pong.

As he watched the concentric circles of ripples fanning out on the dark surface of the stream, Quellen became conscious again of the warning bell ringing again at the other end of the house. *Pong. Pong. Pong.* The uneasiness within him turned to sullen foreboding. He eased himself out of his chair and headed hurriedly toward the phone. *Pong.*

Quellen switched it on, leaving the vision off. It hadn't been easy to arrange things so that any calls coming to his home, back in Appalachia half a world away, were automatically relayed to him here.

"Quellen," he said, eyeing the gray blank screen.

"Koll speaking," came the crackling reply. "Couldn't reach you before. Why don't you turn on your visi, Quellen?"

"It's not working," Quellen said. He hoped sharp-nosed Koll, his immediate superior at the Secretariat of Crime, would not smell the lie in his voice.

"Get over here quickly, will you, Quellen? Spanner and I have something urgent to take up with you. Got it, Quellen? Urgent. It's a High Government matter. They're treading us hard."

"Yes, sir. Anything else, sir?"

"No. We'll fill in the details for you when you get here. Which will be at once." Koll decisively snapped the contact.

Quellen stared at the blank screen for a while, chewing at his lip. Terror clawed his soul. Was this it, the summons to headquarters to discuss his highly illegal, criminally selfish hideaway? Had the downfall come at last? No. No. They *couldn't* have found out. It was impossible. He had everything squared.

But, came Quellen's insistent thought, they must have discovered his secret. Why else would Koll send for him so urgently, with the whiplash tone in his voice? Quellen began to perspire despite the air conditioning, which kept away most of the fierce Congo heat.

They would put him back in Class Eight if they found out. Or, much more likely, they would bounce him all the way back to Twelve or Thirteen, and slap a perpetual hold on him. He would be doomed to spend the rest of his life in a tiny room inhabited by two or three other people, the biggest, smelliest, most unpleasant people the clicking computers could find for him.

Quellen calmed himself. Perhaps he was taking alarm for no reason. Koll had said it was High Government business, hadn't he? A directive from above, not any private arrest. When they really found him out, Quellen knew, they wouldn't simply summon him. They would *come* for him. So this was some affair of work. He had a momentary vision of the members of the High Government, shadowy demigods at least eleven feet high, pausing in their incomprehensible labors to drop a minislip memo down the chute to Koll.

Quellen took a long look at the green overhanging trees, bowed under the weight of their leaves and glistening with the beaded drops of the morning's rain. He let his eyes rove regretfully over the two spacious rooms, his luxurious porch, the uncluttered view. Each time he left here, it was as though for the last time. For a moment, now that everything might well be just about lost, Quellen almost relished the buzzing of the flies. He gulped in a final sweeping look and stepped toward the stat. The purple field enveloped him. He was sucked into the machine.

Quellen was devoured. The hidden power generators of the stat were connected by direct link to the central generator that spun endlessly on its poles at the bottom of the Atlantic, condensing the theta force that made the stat travel possible. What was theta force? Quellen could not say. He could barely explain electricity, and that had been around for a longer time. He took it for granted and gave himself to the stat field. If someone had introduced a minor abscissa distortion, Quellen's atoms would be broadcast to the universe and never reassembled, but one did not think about such things.

The effect was instantaneous. The lean, lanky form of Quellen was shattered, a stream of tagged wavicles was relayed halfway across the planet, and Quellen was reconstituted. It happened so fast—molecule ripped from molecule in a fragment of a nanosecond—that his neural system could not pick up the pain of total dissolution. The restoration of life came just as swiftly.

One did not think about the realities of stat travel. One simply traveled. To do otherwise was to ask for the miseries.

Quellen emerged in the tiny apartment for Class Seven citizens of Appalachia that everyone thought he inhabited. Some messages awaited him. He glanced at them: they were advertising blares mainly, although a note told him that his sister Helaine had come calling. Quellen felt a twitch of guilt. Helaine and her husband were prolets of the prole, ground under by the harsh realities. He had often wished he could do something for them, since their unhappiness added prongs to his own sense of conscience. Yet what could he do? He preferred not to get involved.

In a series of swift motions he slipped out of his lounging clothes and into his crisp business uniform, and removed the *Privacy* radion from the door. Thus he transformed himself from Joe Quellen, owner of an illegal privacy-nest in the heart of an unreported reservation in

Africa, into Joseph Quellen, CrimeSec, staunch defender of law and order. He left the house. The elevator tumbled him endless stories to the tenth-floor quickboat landing. Stat transmission within a city was technically impossible; more's the pity, Quellen felt.

A quickboat slid onto its ramp. Quellen joined the multitudes pressing into it. He felt the thrum of power as it moved outward. Aching numbly from fear, Quellen headed downtown to meet Koll.

The building of Secretariat of Crime was considered an architectural masterpiece, Quellen had been told. Eighty stories, topped by spiked towers, and the crimson curtain-walls were rough and sandy in texture, so that they sparkled like a beacon when illuminated. The building had roots; Quellen had never learned how many underlevels there were, and he suspected that no one really knew, save certain members of the High Government. Surely there were twenty levels of computer down there, and a crypt for dead storage below that, and a further eight levels of interrogation rooms even deeper. Of that much, Quellen had sure knowledge. Some said that there was another computer, forty levels thick, underneath the interrogation rooms, and there were those who maintained that this was the true computer, while the one above was only for decoration and camouflage. Perhaps. Quellen did not try to probe too deeply into such things. For all he knew, the High Government itself met in secret councils a hundred levels below street level in this very building. He kept his curiosity under check. He did not wish to invite the curiosity of others, and that meant placing a limit on his own.

Clerical workers nodded respectfully to Quellen as he passed between their close-packed rows. He smiled. He could afford to be gracious; here he had status, the *mana* of Class Seven. They were Fourteens, Fifteens, the boy emptying the disposal basket was probably a Twenty. To them, he was a lofty figure, virtually a confidant of High Government people, a personal associate of Danton and Kloofman themselves, All a matter of perspective, Quellen thought. Actually he had glimpsed Danton—or someone said to be Danton—only once. He had no real reason to think that Kloofman actually existed, though probably he did.

Clamping his hand vigorously on the doorknob, Quellen waited to be scanned. The door of the inner office opened. He entered and found unfriendly figures hunched at desks within. Little sharp-nosed Martin Koll, looking for all the world like some huge rodent, sat facing the door, sifting through a sheaf of minislips. Leon Spanner, Quellen's other boss, sat opposite him at the glistening table, his great bull neck hunching over still more memoranda. As Quellen came into the room, Koll reached to the wall with a quick nervous gesture and flipped up the oxy vent, admitting a supply for three.

"Took you long enough," Koll said, without looking up.

Quellen glowered at him. Koll was gray-haired, gray-faced, gray of soul. Quellen hated him. "Sorry," he said. "I had to change. I was off duty."

"Whatever we do won't alter anything," rumbled Spanner, as if no one had entered and nothing had been said. "What's happened has happened, and nothing we do will have the slightest effect. Do you see? It makes me want to smash things! To pound and break!"

"Sit down, Quellen," Koll said offhandedly. He turned to Spanner, a big, beefy man with a furrowed forehead and thick features. "I thought we'd been through this all before," Koll said. "If we meddle it's going to mix up everything. With about five hundred years to cover, we'll scramble the whole framework. That much is clear."

Quellen silently breathed relief. Whatever it was they were concerned about, it wasn't his illegal African hideaway. From the way it sounded, they were talking about the time-hoppers. Good. He looked at his two superiors more carefully, now that his eyes were no longer blurred by fear and the anticipation of humiliating punishment. They had obviously been arguing quite a while, Koll and Spanner. Koll was the deep one, with his agile mind and nervous, birdlike energy. But Spanner had more power. They said he had connections in high places, even High places.

"All right, Koll," Spanner grunted. "I'll even grant that it will mix up the past. I'll concede that much."

"Well, that's something," the small man said.

"Don't interrupt me. I still think we've got to put a stop to it. We can't undo what's done, but we can cut it short this year. In fact, we must."

Koll glared balefully at Spanner. Quellen could see that his own presence was the only reason Koll was concealing the anger lying just behind his eyes. They would be spew-

15

ing curses at one another if the underling Quellen did not happen to be in the room.

"Why, Spanner, why?" Koll demanded in what passed for measured tones. "If we keep the process going we maintain things as they are. Four thousand of them went in '86, nine thousand in '87, fifty thousand in '88. And when we get last year's figures, they'll be even higher. Look—here it says that over a million hoppers arrived in the first eighty years, and after that the figures kept rising. Think of the population we're losing! It's wonderful! We can't *afford* to let these people stay here, when we have a chance to get rid of them. And when history says that we did get rid of them."

"History also says that they stopped going back to the past after 2491. Which means that we caught them next year," Spanner said. "I mean, that we *will* catch them next year. It's ordained. We've got no choice but to obey. The past's a closed book."

"Is it?" Koll laughed; it was almost a bark. "What if we don't solve it? What if the hoppers keep on going back?"

"It didn't happen that way, though. We *know* it. All the hoppers who reached the past came from the years 2486 to 2491. That's a matter of record," said Spanner doggedly.

"Records can be falsified."

"The High Government wants this traffic stopped. Why must I argue with you, Koll? You want to defy history, that's your business, but defying Them as well? No. We don't have that option."

"But to clear away millions of prolets—"

Spanner grunted and tightened his grasp on the minislips he was holding. Quellen, feeling like an intruder, let his eyes flick back from one man to the other.

"All right," Spanner said slowly. "I'll agree with you that it's nice to keep losing all those prolets. Even though on the face of things it appears that we won't go on losing them much longer. You say we have to let it keep going on, or else it'll alter the past. I take the opposite view. But let that pass. I won't argue the point, since you seem so positive. Furthermore, you think that it's a good thing to use this time-hopper business as a method of reducing population. I'm with you on that too, Koll. I don't like overcrowding any more than you do, and I'll admit things have reached a ridiculous state nowadays. But consider: we're being hoodwinked. For someone to be running a

16

time-travel business behind our backs is illegal and unethical and a lot of other things, and he ought to be stopped. What do you say, Quellen? Ultimately this is going to be the responsibility of your department, you know."

The sudden reference to him came as a jolt. Quellen was still struggling to get his bearings in this debate, and he was not entirely sure what they were talking about. He smiled weakly and shook his head.

"No opinion?" Koll asked abrasively.

Quellen looked at him. He was unable to stare straight into Koll's hard, colorless eyes, and so he let his gaze rest on the bureau manager's cheekbones instead. He remained silent.

"No opinion, Quellen? That's too bad indeed. It doesn't speak well of you."

Quellen repressed a shudder. "I'm afraid that I haven't been keeping up with the latest developments in the timehopper case. As you know, I've been very busy on certain projects that—"

He let his voice trail off, feeling like a fool. His eager assistants probably knew all about this situation, he thought. He wondered why he had never bothered to check with Brogg. But how could he anticipate everything?

Koll said, "Are you aware that thousands of prolets have vanished into nowhere since the beginning of the year, Quellen?"

"No, sir. Ah, I mean, of course, sir. Certainly. It's just that we haven't really had a chance to take action on it," Quellen said.

The footling sound of his own voice appalled him. *Very lame, Quellen, very lame,* he told himself. *Of course you don't know anything about it, when you spend all your free time in that pretty little hideaway across the ocean. But Stanley Brogg probably knows every detail. Brogg is very efficient.*

"Well, just where do you think they've gone?" Koll asked. "Maybe you think they've all hopped into stats and gone off somewhere to look for work? To Africa, maybe?"

The barb had poison on it. Quellen came close to gasping in shock before he could convince himself that Koll was stabbing in the dark. He hid his reaction as well as he could and replied evenly, "I have no idea, sir."

"You haven't been reading your history books very

well, then, Quellen. Think, man: what was the most important historical development of the past five centuries?"

Quellen thought. What, indeed? The Entente? The coming of the High Government? The breakdown of the nations? The stat? He hated the way Koll could turn him into an idiotic schoolboy. Quellen knew he was no fool, however inane he might seem when hauled on the carpet. He was competent enough. But at the core of his being was his vulnerability, his hidden crime, and that meant he was jelly at the core. He began to sweat. He said, "I'm not sure how to evaluate that question, sir."

Koll casually flipped the oxy up a little higher, in an almost insulting gesture of friendliness. The sweet gas purred into the room. Softly Koll said, "I'll tell you, then. It's the arrival of the hoppers. And *this* is the era they're starting out from."

"Of course," Quellen said. Everyone knew about the hoppers, and he was annoyed with himself for not simply offering the obvious to Koll.

"Someone's developed time travel in the past few years," Spanner said. "He's beginning to siphon the time-hoppers back to the past. Thousands of unemployed prolets are gone already, and if we don't catch him soon he'll clutter up the past with every wandering workingman in the country."

"So? That's just my point," Koll said impatiently. "We know they've already arrived in the past; our history books say so. Now we can sit back and let this fellow distribute our refuse all over the previous five centuries."

Spanner swiveled round and confronted Quellen. "What do you think?" he demanded. "Should we follow the order of the High Government, round up this fellow, and stop the departure of the hoppers? Or should we do as Koll says and let everything go on, which defies not only Them but also incidentally the information of history?"

"I'll need time to study the case," Quellen said suspiciously. The last thing that he wanted to have happen to him was to be forced into making a judgment in favor of one superior over another.

"Let me show you your path right now," Spanner said, with a side glance at Koll. "We have our instructions from the High Government, and it's futile to debate them. As Koll here knows quite well, Kloofman himself has taken an interest in this case. Our task is to locate the illegal nexus of time-travel activity and bring it under official control. Koll, if you object, you'd better appeal to the High Government."

"No objections," said Koll. "Quellen?"

Quellen stiffened. "Yes, sir?"

"You heard Mr. Spanner. Get on it, fast. Track down this fellow who's shipping the hoppers and put him away, but not before you get his secret out of him. The High Government wants control of the process. And a halt to this illegal activity. It's all yours, Quellen."

He was dismissed.

two

Norman Pomrath looked coldly at his wife and said, "When is your brother going to do something for us, Helaine?"

"I've told you. He can't."

"He won't, you mean."

"He *can't*. Who do you think he is, Danton? And will you please get out of my way? I need a shower."

"At least you said please," Pomrath grumbled. "I'm grateful for small mercies."

He stepped to one side. Out of some tatter of modesty he did not watch as his wife stripped off her green tunic. She crumpled the garment, tossed it aside, and got under the molecular bath. Since she stood with her back to him while she washed, he let himself watch her. Modesty was an important thing, Pomrath thought. Even when you've been married eleven years, you've got to give the other person some privacy in these stinking one-room lives. Otherwise you'll click your gyros. He gnawed a fingernail and stole furtive glances at his wife's lean buttocks.

The air in the Pomrath apartment was foul, but he didn't dare turn up the oxy. He had drawn this week's supply, and if he nudged the stud, the utility computer somewhere in the bowels of the earth would say unpleasant things to him. Pomrath didn't think his nerves could stand much garbage from a utility computer just now. His nerves couldn't stand much of anything. He was Class Fourteen, which was bad enough, and he hadn't had any work in three months, which was worse, and he had a brother-in-law in Class Seven, which really cut into him. What good did Joe Quellen do him, though? The damned guy was never around. Ducking out on his family responsibilities.

Helaine was finished with her shower. The molecular bath used no water; only Class Ten and up was entitled to use water for purposes of bodily cleaning. Since most people in the world were Class Eleven and down, the planet would stink halfway across the universe but for the handy molecular baths. You stripped down, stood in front of the nozzle, and ultrasonic waves cunningly separated the grime from your skin and gave you the illusion of being clean. Pomrath did not bother to avert his eyes as Helaine's nude white form crossed in front of him. She wriggled into her tunic. Once, he remembered, he had thought that she was voluptuous. He had been much younger then. Later, it had seemed to him that she had begun to lose weight. Now she was thin. There were times—especially at night—when she hardly looked female to him.

He slid down into the webfoam cradle along one windowless wall and said, "When do the kids get home?"

"Fifteen minutes. That's why I showered now. Are you staying here, Norm?"

"I'm going out in five minutes."

"To the sniffer palace?"

He scowled at her. His face, creased and pleated by defeat, was well designed for scowling. "No," he said, "not to the sniffer palace. To the job machine."

"But you know the job machine will contact you here if there's any work, so—"

"I want to go to *it*," Pomrath said with icy dignity. "I do not want it to come to *me*. I will go to the job machine. And then, most likely to the sniffer palace afterward. Perhaps to celebrate and perhaps to drown my sorrow."

"I knew it."

"Damn you, Helaine, why don't you get off me? Is it my fault I'm between jobs? I rank high in skills. I ought to be working. But there's a cosmic injustice in the universe that keeps me unemployed."

She laughed harshly. The harshness was a new note, something of the last few years "You've had work exactly twenty-three weeks in eleven years," she told him. "The rest of the time we've collected doles. You've moved up from Class Twenty to Class Fourteen, and there you stick, year after year, and we're getting nowhere, and the walls of this damned apartment are like a cage to me, and when those two kids are in it with me I feel like tearing their heads off, and—"

"Helaine," he said quietly. "Stop it."

To his considerable surprise, she did. A muscle knotted in her jaw as she caught herself headlong in her stream of protest. Much more calmly she said, "I'm sorry, Norm. It's not your fault we're prolets. There are only so many jobs to be had. Even with your skills—"

"Yes. I know."

"It's the way things are. I didn't mean to screech, Norm. I love you, do you know that? For better, for worse, like they say."

"Sure, Helaine. All right."

"Maybe I'll go to the sniffer palace with you, this time. Let me get the kids programmed and—"

He shook his head. It was very touching, this sudden display of affection, but he saw enough of Helaine in the apartment, day and night. He didn't want her following him around as he took his pitiful pleasures. "Not this time, sweeting," he said quickly. "Remember, I've got to go punch the job machine first. You'd better stay here. Go visit Beth Wisnack, or somebody."

"Her husband's still gone."

"Who, Wisnack? Haven't they traced him?"

"They think he—he hopped. I mean, they've had a televector on him and everything," Helaine said. "No trace. He's really gone."

"You believe in this hopper business?" Pomrath asked.

"Of course."

"Traveling in time? It doesn't make any sense. I mean, as a matter of teleology, if you start turning the universe upside down, if you confuse the direction in which events flow, Helaine, I mean—"

Her eyes were very wide. "The faxtapes say there's such a thing. The High Government is investigating it. Joe's own department. Norm, how can you say there are no time-hoppers, when people are disappearing every day? When Bud Wisnack right on the next level—"

"There's no proof he did that."

"Where else is he, then?"

"Antarctica, maybe. Poland. Mars. A televector can slip up just like anybody else. I can't swallow this time-travel deal, Helaine. It has no thingness for me, do you follow? It's unreal, a fantasy, something out of a sniffer dream."

22

Pomrath coughed. He was doing a lot of vociferous talking lately. He thought about Bud Wisnack, small and bald, with an eternal blue stubble on his cheeks, and wondered if he had really jumped a hoop in time and gone off to 1999 or whenever.

The Pomraths looked at each other in awkward silence for a moment. Then Helaine said, "Tell me something hypothetical, Norm. If you went outside now and a man came up to you and said he was running the hopper business, and did you want to go back in time and get away from it all, what would you say to him?"

Pomrath considered. "I'd tell him no. I mean, would it be honorable to skip out on my wife and family? It's all right for a Bud Wisnack, but I couldn't duck all my responsibilities, Helaine."

Her gray-blue eyes sparkled. She smiled her don't-fool-me-kiddo smile. "That's very nobly said, Norm. But I think you'd go, all the same."

"You're entitled to think what you want to think. Since it's all a fantasy anyway, it doesn't really matter. I'm going to have a look at the job machine now. I'll give it a real punch. Who knows? I might find myself twitched right up to Class Seven with Joe."

"Could be," Helaine said. "What time will you be back?"

"Later."

"Norm, don't spend too much time at the sniffer palace. I hate it when you get high on that stuff."

"I'm the masses," he told her. "I need my opium."

He palmed the door. It slid open with a little whickering sound, and he went out. The hall light was burning feebly. Cursing, Pomrath groped his way toward the elevator. The hall lights weren't like this in Class Seven places, he knew. He had visited Joe Quellen. Not often, true; his brother-in-law didn't mingle much with the prolets, even when they were his own kin. But he had seen. Quellen led a damned good life. And what was he, anyway? What were his skills? He was just a bureaucrat, a papershuffler. There was nothing Joe Quellen could do that a computer couldn't do better. But he had a job. Tenure.

Gloomily Pomrath stared at his distorted reflection in the burnished framework of the elevator oval. He was a squat, broadshouldered man just past forty, with heavy eyebrows and tired, sad eyes. The reflection made him look older, with much flesh at his throat. Give me time, he thought. He stepped through the oval and was sped upward toward the surface level of the huge apartment house.

I made my choices of my own free will, he insisted. I married the voluptuous Helaine Quellen. I had my permitted two children. I opted for my kind of work. And here I am in one room for four people, and my wife is skinny and I don't look at her when she's naked because I have to spare her nerves, and the oxy quota is used up, and here I am going to punch the job machine and find out the old, old story, and then to drop a lousy few pieces at the sniffer palace, and—

Pomrath wondered what exactly he would do if some agent of the time-hopper people came up to him and offered to peddle him a ticket into a quieter yesterday. Would he do a Bud Wisnack and grab at the chance?

This is nonsense, Pomrath told himself. Such an option doesn't exist. The time-hoppers are imaginary. A fraud perpetrated by the High Government. You can't travel backward in time. All you can do is go relentlessly forward, at a rate of one second per second.

But if that's the case, Norm Pomrath asked himself, where did Bud Wisnack really go?

When the apartment door closed, and Helaine found herself alone, she slumped down wearily on the edge of the all-purpose table in the middle of the room and bit down hard on her lower lip to keep back the tears.

He didn't even notice me, she thought. I took a shower right in front of him and he didn't even notice.

Actually, Helaine had to admit, that wasn't true. She had watched his reflection in the coppery wall-plate that was their substitute for a window, and she had seen him covertly looking at her body as she stood with her back to him under the shower. And then, when she had walked naked across the room to pick up her tunic, he had looked at her again, the front view.

But he hadn't *done* anything. That was the essential thing. If he felt some spark of sexual feeling for her, he would have showed it. With a caress, a smile, a hasty hand slammed against the button that would bring the hidden bed sliding out of the wall. He had looked at her body, and it hadn't had any effect on him at all. Helaine suffered more from that than from all the rest.

She was thirty-seven, almost. That wasn't really old. She

24

had seventy or eighty years of actuarial lifespan ahead of her. Yet she felt middle-aged. She had lost a great deal of weight lately, so that her hip-bones jutted out like misplaced shoulderblades. She no longer wore her off-the-bosom dresses. She knew that she had ceased to have much sensual appeal for her husband, and it pained her.

Was it true, the stories going around that the High Government was promoting special anti-sex measures? That by order of Danton the men were getting impotence pills and the women were receiving desensualizers? That was what the women were whispering. Noelle Kalmuck said that the laundry-room computer had told her so. You had to believe what a computer told you, didn't you? Presumably the machine was plugged right into the High Government itself.

But it made no sense. Helaine was no genius, but she had common sense. Why would the High Government want to meddle with the sex drive? Surely not as a birth-control measure. They controlled birth more humanely, by interfering with fertility, not with potency. Two children per married couple, that was *it*. If they allowed only one, they might be making some headway with the population problem, but unfortunately there were substantial pressure groups who insisted on the two-child family, and even the High Government had bowed. So population was stabilized, and even reduced a little—taking into account the bachelors, like Helaine's brother Joe, and the couples who had sworn the Sterility Pledge, and such—but no real headway was made.

Still, with fertility controlled, it was illogical for the High Government to take away sex as well. Sex was the sport of the prolets. It was free. You didn't need to have a job in order to enjoy sex. It passed the time. Helaine decided that the rumors she had heard were sheer foolishness, and she doubted that the laundry computer had said anything on the subject to Noelle Kalmuck. Why should the computer talk to Noelle at all? She was just a giggly little fool.

Of course, you could never tell. The High Government could be devious. This time-hopper business, for example: was there any truth in it, Helaine wondered? Well, there were all the accredited documents of time-hoppers who had arrived in previous centuries, but suppose they were all frauds inserted in the history books simply to baffle and confuse? What was the real and what was imagined?

Helaine sighed. "What time is it?" she asked.

Her earwatch said gently, "Ten minutes to fifteen."

The children would be arriving home from school soon. Little Joseph was seven, Marina was nine. At this age, they still had some shreds of innocence, as much as any children could have who spent all their lives in the same room as their parents. Helaine turned to the foodbox and programmed their afternoon snack with furious jabs of her knuckles. She had just finished the job when the children appeared.

They greeted her. Helaine shrugged. "Plug in and have your snacks," she said.

Joseph grinned angelically at her. "We saw Kloofman in school today. He looks like Daddy."

"Sure," Helaine said. "The High Government has nothing better to do than visit schoolrooms, I know. And the reason why Kloofman looks like Daddy is—" She cut herself short. She had been about to say something untrue, but Joseph had a literal mind. He'd repeat it, and the next day the investigators would come around to know why the Class Fourteen Pomrath family was claiming to be related to one of Them.

Marina broke in, "It wasn't really Kloofman anyway. Not himself. They just showed pictures of him on the wall." She nudged her brother. "Kloofman wouldn't come to your grade, silly. He's much too busy."

"Marina's right," Helaine said. "Listen, children, I've programmed you. Have your snack and start your homework right away."

"Where's Daddy?" Joseph asked.

"He went to punch the job machine."

"Will he get a job today?" Marina wanted to know.

"It's hard to say." Helaine smiled evasively. "I'm going to visit Mrs. Wisnack."

The children ate. Helaine stepped through the door and went uplevel to the Wisnack apartment. The door told her that Beth was home, so Helaine announced herself and was admitted. Beth Wisnack nodded to her wordlessly. She looked terribly tired. She was a small woman, just about forty, with dark, trusting eyes and dull-green hair pulled back in a tight grip to a bun. Her two children, the usual boy and girl, sat with their backs to the door, snacking.

"Any news?" Helaine asked.

"None. None. He's gone, Helaine. They won't admit it

yet, but he's hopped, and he won't ever come back. I'm a widow."

"What about the televector search?"

The little woman shrugged. "According to law they've got to keep it going eight days. Then that's all. They've searched the registered list of hoppers, but there's nobody named Wisnack on it. Which doesn't mean a thing, of course. Very few of them used their real names when they arrived in the past. And the early ones, they didn't even record the physical descriptions. So there'll be no proof. But he's gone. I'm applying for my pension next week."

Helaine felt the weight of Beth Wisnack's misery like some kind of additional humidity in the room. Her heart went out to her. Life wasn't very attractive here in Class Fourteen, but at least you had your family structure to cling to in times of stress. Beth didn't even have that, now. Her husband had put thumb to nose and disappeared on a one-way journey to the past. "Good-by, Beth, good-by, kids, good-by, lousy twenty-fifth century," he might have said, as he vanished down the time tunnel. The coward couldn't face responsibility, Helaine thought. And who was going to marry Beth Wisnack now?

"I feel so sorry for you," Helaine murmured.

"Save it. There'll be troubles for you, too. All the men will run away. You'll see. Norm will go too. They talk big about obligations, but then they run. Bud swore he'd never go, either. But he was out of work two years, you know, and even with the check every week he couldn't stand it any more. So he went."

Helaine didn't like the implication that her own husband was about to check out. It seemed ungracious of Beth to hurl such a wish at her, even in her own grief. After all, Helaine thought, I came on a simple neighborly mission of consolation. Beth's words hadn't been kind.

Beth seemed to realize it.

"Sit down," she said. "Rest. Talk to me. I tell you, Helaine, I hardly know what's real any more, since the night Bud didn't come back. I only wish you're spared this kind of torture."

"You mustn't give up hope yet," Helaine said gently.

Empty words, Helaine knew. Beth Wisnack knew it too.

Maybe I'll talk to my brother Joe, she thought. See him again. Maybe there's something he can do for us. He's Class Seven, an important man.

God, I don't want Norm to become a hopper!

three

Quellen was glad to escape from Koll and Spanner. Once he was back in his own office, behind his own small but private desk. Quellen could feel his status again. He was something more than a flunky, no matter how Koll chose to push him around.

He rang for Brogg and Leeward, and the two Under-Secs appeared almost instantly.

"Good to see you again," Stanley Brogg said sourly. He was a large man, somber-looking, with a heavy face and thick, hairy-backed fingers. Quellen nodded to him and reached out to open the oxy vent, letting the stuff flow into the office and trying to capture the patronizing look Koll had flashed at him while doing the same thing fifteen minutes before. Brogg did not look awed. He was only Class Nine, but he had power over Quellen, and both of them knew it.

Leeward did not look awed either, for different reasons. Leeward simply was not sensitive to small gestures. He was a towering, cadaverous, undemonstrative man who went about his work in a routinely methodical way. Not a dolt, but destined never to get out of Class Nine, either.

Quellen surveyed his two assistants. He could not bear the silent scrutiny he was getting from Brogg. Brogg was the one who knew the secret of the African hideaway; a third of Quellen's substantial salary was the price that kept Brogg quiet about Quellen's second, secret home. Big Leeward did not know and did not care; he took his orders directly from Brogg, not from Quellen, and blackmail was not his specialty.

"I suppose you've been informed of our assignment to

handle the recent prolet disappearances," Quellen began. "The so-called time-hoppers have become the problem of the Secretariat of Crime, as we have anticipated for several years now."

Brogg produced a thick stack of minislips. "As a matter of fact, I was going to get in touch with you about the situation just now. The High Government's taken quite an interest. Koll no doubt has told you that Kloofman himself is involved. I have the new statistics. In the first four months of this year sixty-eight thousand prolets have vanished."

"But you're on the case?"

"Of course," Brogg said.

"Progress report?"

"Well," Brogg said, pacing up and down the little room and wiping the sweat from his heavy jowls, "you know the theory, though it's been occasionally controverted. That the hoppers are starting out from our proximate time-nexus. I've plotted it all. Tell him, Leeward."

Leeward said, "A statistical distribution shows that the theory is correct. The present disappearances of prolets are linked directly to historical records of the appearance of the so-called hoppers in the late twentieth century and succeeding years."

Brogg pointed to a blue-covered volume lying on Quellen's desk. "History spool. I put it there for you. It confirms my findings. The theory's sound."

Quellen ran a finger along his jawline and wondered what it was like to carry around as much fat on one's face as Brogg did. Brogg was perspiring heavily, and his expression was a sad one; he was virtually begging Quellen with his eyes to open the oxy vent wider. The moment of superiority pleased the harried CrimeSec, and he made no move toward the wall.

Crisply Quellen said, "All you've done is to confirm the obvious. We know the hoppers have been taking off from this approximate era. That's been a fact of record since roughly 1979. The High Government directive orders us to isolate the distribution vector. I've developed an immediate course of action."

"Which has been approved by Koll and Spanner, of course," Brogg said insolently. His jowls quivered as his voice rumbled through them.

"It has," Quellen said with as much force as he could muster. It angered him that Brogg could so easily deflate him. Koll, yes, Spanner, yes—but Brogg was supposed to be his assistant. Brogg knew too much about him, though. Quellen said, "I want you to track down the slyster who's shipping these hoppers back. Do anything within the codes to halt his illegal activity. Bring him here. I want him caught before he sends anyone else into the past."

"Yes, sir," Brogg said with unaccustomed humility. "We'll work on it. Which is to say, we'll continue our already established line of exploration. We have tracers out in various prolet strata. We're doing all we can to pull in a lead. We think it's only a matter of time now. A few days. A week. The High Government will be satisfied."

"Let's hope so," Quellen snapped, and dismissed them.

He activated a view-window and peered at the street far below. It seemed to him that he could make out the distant figures of Brogg and Leeward as they appeared on the street, jostled their way to a belt, and disappeared among the multitudes that thronged the outdoor environment. Turning away, Quellen reached for the oxy vent with almost savage joy and flipped it to its widest. He leaned back. Hidden fingers in his chair massaged him. He looked at the book Brogg had left for him, and thumbed his eyeballs wearily.

Hoppers!

It was inevitable, he realized, that this would be dumped on him. All the odd things were, the scrawny conspiracies against law and order. Four years ago, it had been that syndicate of bootlegged artificial organs. Quellen shuddered. Defective pancreases peddled in pestilent alleyways, throbbing blood-filled hearts, endless coils of gleaming intestines, marketed by shady slysters who flitted noiselessly from zone to zone. And then it had been the fertility bank and the grubby business of the sperm withdrawals. And then the alleged creatures from the adjoining universe who had run through the streets of Appalachia clashing hideous red mandibles and clutching at children with scaly claws. Quellen had handled those things, not brilliantly, for brilliance was not his style, but competently, at least.

And now hoppers.

The assignment unsettled him. He had haggled for secondhand kidneys and he had quibbled over the price of ova, all in a day's work, but he did not like this business of coping with illegal time-travel. The framework of the cosmos seemed to warp a little, once you admitted the possibility that such a thing could occur. It was bad enough that time kept flowing relentlessly forward; a man could understand that, though he did not necessarily have to like it. Backward, though? A reversal of all logic, a denial of all reason? Quellen was a reasonable man. Time paradoxes troubled him. How easy it would be, he knew, to step into the seat and leave Appalachia behind, return to the tranquil humidity of his African hideaway, shrug off all responsibility.

He conquered the creeping apathy that beset him and snapped on the projector. Stereoscopic Julesz figures flashed on the screen while his eyes adjusted to undifferentiated blacks and whites. The Julesz edge kept the screen perpetually in focus, no matter what the degree of optical distortion. The history spool began to unroll. Quellen watched the words, sharp as blades, stream by:

The first sign of invasion from the future came about the year 1979, when several men in strange costumes appeared in the district of Appalachia then known as Manhattan. Records show they appeared with increasing frequency throughout the next decade, and when interrogated all ultimately admitted that they had come from the future. The pressure of repeated evidence eventually forced the people of the twentieth century to accept the disturbing conclusion that they were in truth being subjected to a peaceful but annoying invasion by time-travelers.

There was more, a whole reel more, but Quellen had had enough for the moment. He cut the projector off. The heat of the little room was oppressive, despite the air conditioning and the oxy vent. He could smell his own acrid sweat and didn't like the sensation. Quellen looked despairingly at the confining walls, thinking with longing of the murky stream that ran by the front porch of his African retreat.

He nudged the pedal stud of the minislip dictator and delivered himself of a few memos:

"1. Can we catch a live hopper? That is, a man from our own time who went back, say, ten or twenty years and has lived on back through his own lifespan a second time? Are there such men? What would happen if one met himself of pre-hop existence?

"2. Assuming capture of a live hopper, apply interrogation techniques to discover source of original backward momentum.

"3. Current indications are that hopper phenomenon ceases as of year 2491. Does this indicate success in our prevention attempts or merely lacunae in the records?.

"4. Is it true that no hoppers were recorded prior to A.D. 1979? Why?

"5. Consider possibility of masquerading as Class Fifteen prolet in order to experience solicitation by hopper-transport agents. Would such an arrest be considered entrapment? Check with legal machines.

"6. Take depositions from families of recently departed prolet hoppers. Sociological index, reliability rating, etc. Also attempt to retrace events leading up to disappearance of hopper.

"7. Perhaps—"

Quellen rejected the last memo in unfinished form and kicked over the pedal. The dictator thrust minislips at him. He let them lie on his desk and started the projector again, reeling out some more of the history spool.

Analysis of the time-hopper records indicates that all reported arrivals took place within the years 1979 and 2106 A.D.—that is, an era prior to the establishment of the High Government. (Quellen made a mental note. Possibly it was significant.) Those hoppers who upon interrogation were willing to admit to a year of departure listed the same as lying between 2486 and 2491 A.D., without exception. Of course, this does not foreclose the possibility of unreported hoppers departing from a time other than that, just as it does not eliminate all possibility that arrivals were not confined wholly to the aforementioned period of 127 years. Nonetheless—

There was an interruption in the text. Brogg had inserted his own memo here:

See Exhibits A, B. Examine possibility of time-travel outside recorded temporal zones. Occult phenomena. Worth study.

Quellen found Exhibits A and B on his desk: two more spools. He did not put them into the projector. Nor did he run the history spool any further just yet. He paused and considered.

All the hoppers seemed to be coming from a single five-year period, of which this was the fourth year. All the hoppers had landed within a temporal spectrum of about a century and a quarter. Naturally, some hoppers had escaped detection, slipping smoothly into the life-patterns of their new era and never showing up on the charts of time-travel. Methods of persona-detection had been fairly primitive three and four hundred years ago, Quellen knew, and it was surprising that so many of the hoppers had actually been found and recorded. Low-order prolets, though, weren't likely to be subtle about concealing themselves in an era to which they were unaccustomed. But surely the syndicate running the hopper business was not sending back only prolets!

Removing the history spool from the projector, Quellen slipped Brogg's Exhibit A into its place and switched the machine on. Exhibit A was uninspiring: nothing less nor more than a census roll of the recorded hoppers. Quellen tuned in on the data in a random way as it flowed past.

BACCALON, ELLIOT V. Detected 4 April 2007, Trenton, New Jersey. Interrogated eleven hours. Declared date of birth 17 May 2464. Skill classification: computer technician fifth grade. Assigned to Camden Hopper Rehabilitation Zone. Transferred to Westvale Polyclinic District 30 February 2011 for therapy. Discharged 11 April 2013. Employed as switching technician 2013-22. Died 7 March 2022, pleurisy and complications.

BLACKHOUSE, MARTIN D. Detected 18 August 2102, Harrisburg, Pennsylvania. Interrogated fourteen minutes. Declared date of birth 10 July 2470, declared date of departure 1 November 2488. Skill classification: computer technician seventh grade. Assigned to West Baltimore Rehabilitation Zone. Released in full capacity 27 October 2102. Employed as computer technician, Internal Revenue Service, 2102-67. Married Lona Walk (q.v.) 22 June 2104. Died 16 May 2187, pneumonia.

BAGROWSKI, EMANUEL. Detected—

Quellen halted the roster as ideas flooded his mind. He

ran ahead to Lona Walk, *q.v.*, and made the interesting discovery that she was a hopper who had landed in 2098, claiming to have been born in 2471 and to have shipped out for the past on 1 November 2488. This, obviously, had been a prearranged rendezvous; boy of eighteen, girl of seventeen, chucking the twenty-fifth century and heading for the past to start a new life together. Yet Martin Backhouse had landed in 2102, and his girlfriend in 2098. Clearly they hadn't planned it that way. Which told Quellen that the hopper-transporting process was not exact in its attainment of destinations. Or, at least, had not been exact a few years ago. That must have been uncomfortable for poor Lona Walk, Quellen thought: to land in the past and then to find that her heart's desire hadn't made it to the same year.

Quellen was quick to devise some grievous hopper tragedies of this sort. Romeo lands in 2100. Juliet in 2025. Heartbroken Romeo comes upon decades-old gravestone of Juliet. Worse yet, youthful Romeo encounters ninety-year-old Juliet. How did Lona Walk spend the four years while waiting for Martin Backhouse to drop into her era? How could she be sure that he would arrive at all? What if she lost faith and married someone else the year before he showed up? What if the four-year gulf had destroyed their love—for by the time he reached the past, she was objectively twenty-one years old, and he was still only eighteen?

Interesting, Quellen thought. No doubt the playwrights of the twenty-second century had a rich time mining this lode of imaginative material. Bombarded with emigrants out of the future, bedeviled by paradoxes, how those ancient ones must have wrinkled their foreheads over these hoppers!

But of course it was nearly four hundred years since any known hoppers had turned up. The whole phenomenon had been forgotten for generations. Only the fact that the hoppers were coming from *now* had revived it. More's the pity, Quellen thought dourly, that it had to be my time in office.

He pondered other aspects of the problem.

Suppose, he speculated, some hoppers had made a good adaptation, settled down, married people of their new era. Not, like Martin Backhouse, marrying other hoppers, but marrying people whose time-lines began four or five hundred years before their own. That way they might well have

34

married their own great-great-great-great-grandmothers. And thus become their own great-great-great-great-grandfathers. What did that do to genetic flow and continuity of the germ plasm?

Then, too, how about the hopper who lands in 2050, gets into a fist-fight with the first man he meets, knocks him to the pavement, kills him—only to discover that he's slain one of his own direct ancestors and broken his own line of descent? Quellen's head ached. Presumably, any hopper who did that would wink out of existence instantly, never having been born in the first place. Where there any records of such occurrences? Make a note, he said to himself. Check every angle of this thing.

He did not think that such paradoxes were possible. He clung firmly to the idea that it was impossible to change the past, because the past was a sealed book, unchangeable. It had already happened. Any manipulation done by a time-traveler was already in the record. Which makes puppets out of us all, Quellen thought gloomily, finding himself down the dead end of determinism. Suppose I went back in time and killed George Washington in 1772? But Washington, we know, lived till 1799. Would that make it impossible for me to kill him in 1772? He scowled. Such inquiries made his mind spin. Brusquely he ordered himself to return to the business at hand, which was to find some way to halt the further flow of hoppers, thus fulfilling the implied deterministic prophecy that there would be no more hoppers going back after 2491 anyway.

Here's a point to consider, he realized:

Many of these hopper records listed the actual date on which a man took off for the past. This Martin Backhouse, for instance; he had skipped out on November 1, 2488. Too late to do anything about that one now, but what if the records listed a hopper who had taken his departure on April 4, 2490? That was next week. If such a person could be put under surveillance, tracked to the hopper-transporting agent, even prevented from going—

Quellen's heart sank. How could someone be prevented from going back in time, if documents hundreds of years old said that he had made it safely to the past? Paradox, again. It might undermine the structure of the universe. If I interfere, Quellen thought, and pull a man out of the matrix just as he's setting forth—

He scanned the endless roster of hoppers that Brogg had compiled for him. With the furtive pleasure of a man who knows he is doing something quite dangerous, Quellen searched for the information he desired. It took him a while. Brogg had arranged the hopper data alphabetically by name, and had not sorted for date of departure or date of arrival. Besides, many of the hoppers had simply refused or neglected to reveal their date of departure except in the most approximate way. And, with the series of dates nearly four-fifths expired by now, Quellen did not have much leeway.

Half an hour of patient searching, though, turned up the man he wanted:

RADANT, CLARK R. Detected 12 May 1987, Brooklyn, New York. Interrogated eight days. Declared date of birth 14 May 2458, declared date of departure ? May 2490. . . .

It didn't give the exact date, but it would do. A close watch would be kept on Clark Radant during the month to come, Quellen resolved. Let's see if he can slip back to 1987 while we watch him!

He punched for Master Files.

"Get me documents on Clark Radant, born May 14, 2458." Quellen snapped.

The huge computer somewhere below the building was designed to give instant response. It did not necessarily give instant satisfaction, however, and the response that Quellen got was less than useful.

"NO RECORD OF CLARK RADANT BORN 14 MAY 2458," came the reply.

"No record? You mean there's no such person?"

"AFFIRMATIVE."

"That's impossible. He's in the hopper records. Check them. He turned up in Brooklyn on May 12, 1987. See if he didn't."

"AFFIRMATIVE. CLARK RADANT LISTED AMONG 1987 ARRIVALS AND 2490 DEPARTURES."

"You see? So you must have some information on him! Why did you tell me there was no record of him, when—"

"POSSIBLY FRAUDULENT HOPPER LISTING IS ONLY ENTRY. NAME ON LIST DOES NOT IMPLY LEGITIMATE EXISTENCE. EXPLORE POSSIBILITY THAT RADANT NAME IS PSEUDONYM."

Quellen nibbled his lower lip. Yes, no doubt of it! "Radant," whoever he might be, had given a phony name when he landed in 1987. Perhaps all the hopper names on the list were pseudonyms. Maybe they were individually instructed to conceal their real names when they arrived, or possibly indoctrinated so that they could not reveal them, even after interrogation. The enigmatic Clark Radant had been interrogated eight days, it said, and he still hadn't offered a name that corresponded to anything in the birth records.

Quellen saw his bold plan fluttering into the discard. He tried again, though. Expecting to search another half hour, he was rewarded with a new lead after only five minutes:

MORTENSEN, DONALD G. Detected 25 December 2088, Boston, Massachusetts. Interrogated four hours. Declared date of birth 11 June 2462, declared date of departure 4 May 2490. . . .

He hoped it had been a merry Christmas in Boston for Donald Mortensen four hundred two years ago. Quellen punched for Master Files again and demanded to know what there was to be known about Donald Mortensen, born 11 June 2462. He was prepared to learn that no such individual was recorded in the voluminous birth annals of that year.

Instead, the computer began to chatter to him about Donald Mortensen—his skill classification, his marital status, his address, his physical description, his health record. Quellen at length had to silence the machine.

Very well. There *was* a Donald Mortensen. He had not—*would* not—bother to use a pseudonym when he showed up in Boston on Christmas Day forty decades ago. *If* he showed up. Quellen consulted the hopper records again and learned that Mortensen had found employment as an automobile service technician (how prehistoric, Quellen thought!) and had married one Donna Brewer in 2091, fathering five children on her (even more prehistoric!) and living on until 2149, when he expired of an unrecorded disease.

Those five children no doubt had had multitudes of offspring themselves, Quellen realized. Thousands of modern-day human beings might be descended from them, including Quellen himself, or some leader of the High Government. Now, if Quellen's minions closed in on Donald Mortensen as the critical day of May 4 arrived, and prevented him from taking off for the year 2088—

He felt hesitant. The sensation of bold determination that had gripped him a few moments before evaporated completely as he considered the consequences of altering Donald Mortensen's chosen path of action.

Perhaps, Quellen thought, I should have a talk with Koll and Spanner about this, first.

four

The job machine—more formally, the Central Employment Register—was located in the grand lobby of a geodesic dome six hundred feet wide. The dome was surfaced
with a platinum spray three molecules thick. Within, along
the walls of the dome, were the external manifestations of
the computer banks, which were located somewhere else.
A busy inanimate mind worked unsleepingly to tally employment opportunities and to match them with qualifica-
tions.

Norm Pomrath took a quickboat to the job machine.
He could have walked, and saved a piece of change at the
expense of an hour of his time, but he chose not to do so.
It was a deliberate squandering. His time was almost
infinit; his cash supply, despite the generosity of the High
Government, was limited. The weekly dole checks that
reached him through the courtesy of Danton and
Kloofman and the other members of the ruling elite
covered all basic expenses for the Pomrath family of four,
but they did not go much beyond those basic expenses.
Pomrath usually conserved his cash. He hated the dole, of
course; but there was little likelihood of his ever getting
regular work, so he accepted the impersonal benevolence
like everyone else. No one starved except through free
will in this world, and even then it took some doing.

There was really no need for Pomrath to have gone to
the machine. Telephone lines linked every apartment with
any computer to which there should be public access. He
could phone to learn of his status; and in any event if
there had been some upward twitch in his job profile, the
machine would have been in contact with him by this

time. He preferred to get out of the house, though. He knew the job machine's answer in advance, so this was merely a ritual, one of the many sustaining rituals that enabled him to cope with the numbing fact that he was a wholly useless human being.

Subfloor scanners hummed as Pomrath stepped into the building. He was checked, monitored, and identified. If he had been on one of the registers of known anarchists, he would not have been permitted to cross the threshold. Clamps emerging from the marble floor would painlessly have secured his limbs until he could be disarmed and removed from the premises. Pomrath meant no harm to the job machine, however. He harbored hostilities, but they were directed against the universe in general. He was too intelligent a man to waste his wrath on computers.

The benevolent faces of Benjamin Danton and Peter Kloofman beamed down on him from the lofty reaches of the geodesic dome. Giant tridim simulacra dangled from the gleaming struts of the huge building. Danton managed to look severe even while he was smiling; Kloofman, who was reputed to be a man of great humanitarian warmth, was a more inviting figure. Pomrath remembered a time about twenty years ago when the public representatives of the High Government had constituted a triumvirate, with Kloofman and two others whose names he had begun to forget. Then one day Danton had appeared and the pictures of the other two were taken down. Doubtless one day Kloofman and Danton both would vanish, and there would be two—or three—or four new faces on the public buildings. Pomrath did not concern himself too deeply with changes in the personnel of the High Government. Like most people, he had some fundamental doubts about the existence of Kloofman and Danton. There was good reason to believe that the computers were running the whole show, and had been for at least a century now. Yet he did not fail to nod his head reverently to the tridims as he entered the job machine building. For all he knew, Danton might actually be watching him out of the cold eyes of that big simulacrum.

The place was crowded. Pomrath walked to the center of the marble floor, and stood for a moment enjoying the buzz and clamor of the machine. To his left was Bank Red, for job transfers. Pomrath had no dealings there; you needed to have a job before you could start negotiating for a transfer. Straight ahead of him was Bank Green, for members of the hard-core unemployed like himself. To his right was Bank Blue, where new members of the labor force filed applications for work. Each of the three banks had a long line in wait. Kids to the right; a bunch of eager-beaver Class Tens to the left, looking for advancement; straight ahead, the dismal legions of the jobless. Pomrath joined the line at Bank Green.

It moved swiftly. No one spoke to him. Wrapped in a cocoon of privacy in the midst of this crowd, Pomrath wondered, as he often did, where his life had been derailed. He had a high I.Q., he knew. Good reflexes. Determination and ambition and flexibility. Why, he could have been Class Eight by now, if the breaks had gone his way.

They hadn't. They never would. He had trained as a medical technician, thinking that illness was a constant even in a well-ordered world, and so there would always be a job for him. Unfortunately, many other young men of his generation had arrived at the same conclusion. As in the arthropod races, Pomrath thought. You picked your favorite lobster with care, judging his abilities and aggressiveness with all the shrewdness at your command. The factors were there to be assessed. The trouble was a lot of other men were just as shrewd as you; if you could isolate a really superior racer, so could they, and the odds had a way of being 11-10 or worse when you got your bet down. If you won, you were just about breaking even. The secret was to find the 50-to-1 shot who could win. But if he could win, he would not carry such fat odds. The universe, thought Pomrath, is not unfair; it simply is not interested.

He had backed the sure thing, and so his reward had been correspondingly slim: a few weeks of work, many months of unemployment. Pomrath was a good technician. He had his skills, and they were at least the equal of those of a genuine doctor of a few centuries ago. Today, real doctors—there weren't many of them—rated Class Three, just below the lower echelon of the High Government. Pomrath, though, as a mere technician, was bogged down in Class Fourteen and all the attendant discomforts, and the only way he could gain slope on the rating curve was to add to his work-experience rating, but there was no work. Or not very much.

What irony, he thought. Joe Quellen, with no skills at all, is a big-deal Class Seven. Private apartment, no less.

And here I am twice as far down the curve. But Quellen was a member of the government—not the High Government, of course, not the policy-making group, just the government—and so Quellen had to have status. They had to put Quellen in one of the higher classes simply so he'd be able to enforce his authority. Pomrath chewed at a ragged fingernail and wondered why he had not had the good sense to think of going into government service.

Then he answered himself: the odds were even worse there. Quellen had had luck. Maybe a little ability too, Pomrath conceded grudgingly. If I had gone into government instead of becoming a medic, I'd probably be a Class Fourteen clerk today, with regular work but no other advantages that I don't have at the present. The universe is not unfair. But it can be terribly consistent sometimes.

Pomrath was at the head of the line, now.

He was confronted by a blank aluminum plate, some two feet square, in the center of whose shiny surface was mounted a circular scanning shield made of pebbled glass. The shield glowed green and Pomrath clasped his hand over it in the old, familiar ritual.

It was not necessary to talk to the job machine. The job machine knew why Pomrath had come, and who he was, and what fate was in store for him. Nevertheless, Pomrath said in his deep, husky voice, "How about a little work, maybe?" and punched the activating stud.

He got his answer speedily.

Something in the wall behind the shiny aluminum plate made a whirring, chittering sound. Probably strictly for effect, Pomrath thought. To make the prolets believe that that machine is really doing something. A little slot opened in the plate and a minislip came rolling out. Pomrath ripped it off and studied it without much interest.

It bore his name, his job classification rating, and the rest of the identifying gibberish that had accreted to him in his journey through the world. Below that in neat block letters was the verdict:

EMPLOYMENT PROGNOSIS CURRENTLY UN-FAVORABLE. WE WILL INFORM YOU AS OPPORTUNITIES FOR GAINFUL EMPLOY DEVELOP. WE URGE PATIENCE AND UNDER-STANDING. TEMPORARY PRESSURES PRE-

42

VENT THE ATTAINMENT OF THE HIGH GOVERNMENT'S FULL EMPLOYMENT QUOTA.

"Too bad," Pomrath murmured. "My sympathy to the High Government."

He placed the minislip in the disposal slot and turned away, shouldering a path through the swarm of emotionless men waiting to get their share of the bad news. So much for the visit to the job machine.

"What time is it?" he asked.

"Half past sixteen," said his earwatch.

"I think I'll drop in at my friendly sniffer palace. Do you think that's a good idea?"

The earwatch wasn't programmed for such responses. For twice the money, you could get one that would really talk to you, would tell you things other than the time. Pomrath did not think he rated such a luxury in these troubled times. He was also not so hungry for companionship that he yearned for the conversation of an earwatch. Still, he knew, there were those who took consolation from such things.

He stepped outside, into the pale sunlight of the spring afternoon.

The sniffer palace he particularly favored was four blocks away. There were plenty of them, dozens within a ten-block radius of the job-machine building, but Pomrath always went to the same one. Why not? They dispensed the same poisons at each one, so the only commodity that distinguished one from the next was personal service. Even an unemployed Class Fourteen likes to know that he's a valued regular client of something, if only a sniffer palace.

Pomrath walked quickly. The streets were crowded; pedestrianism was in fashion again lately. The short, heavy-set Pomrath had little patience for the obstacles in his way. In fifteen minutes he was at the sniffer palace. It was on the fortieth underlevel of a commercial tank building; by law, all such places of illusion-peddling had to be underground, so that impressionable children at street level would not be prematurely corrupted. Pomrath entered the tank and took the express dropshaft. With great dignity he descended five hundred feet. The tank had eighty levels, terminating in an undertrack that linked it to several adjoining buildings, but Pomrath had never been down that deep to see. He left such subterranean adventures to the members of the High Government, and had no wish to come face to face with Danton somewhere in the depths of the earth.

The sniffer palace had gaudy, somewhat defective argon lights out front. Most such establishments were all-mechanical, but this one had human attendants. That was why Pomrath liked it. He walked in, and there was good old Jerry just within the door, scanning him out of authentic, bloodshot human eyes.

"Norm. Good to see."

"I'm not so sure about that. Business?"

"Lousy. Have a mask."

"Glad to," Pomrath said. "The wife? You got her pregnant yet?"

The plump man behind the counter smiled. "Would I do a crazy thing like that? In a Class Fourteen, do I need a house full of kids? I took the Sterility Pledge, Norm. You forget that?"

"I guess I did," Pomrath said. "Well, okay. There are times I wish I'd done the same. Give me the mask."

"What are you sniffing?"

"Butyl mercaptan," he said at random.

"Come off it. You know we don't—"

"Pyruvic acid, then. With a jolt of lactate dehydrogenase 5 as a spike."

Pomrath drew laughter, but it was mechanical, the laughter of an entrepreneur humoring a valued if slightly embittered customer. "Here, Norm. Stop contaminating my brain and take this. And sweet dreams. You got couch nine, and you owe me a piece and a half."

Taking the mask, Pomrath dropped a few coins into the fleshy palm and retreated to a vacant couch. He kicked his shoes off. He stretched out. He clasped the mask to his face and inhaled. A harmless pastime, a mild hallucinatory gas, a quick illusion to enliven the day. As he went under, Pomrath felt electrodes sliding into place against his skull. To serve as wardens for his alpha rhythms, was the official explanation; if his illusion got too violent, he could be awakened by the management before he did some harm to himself. Pomrath had heard that the electrodes served another, more sinister purpose: to record the hallucinations, to tape them for the benefit of Class Two millionaires who liked the vicarious kick of sitting inside a prolet's mind for a while. Pomrath had asked Jerry about that, but Jerry had denied it. As well he might do. It hardly mattered, Pomrath thought, if the sniffer palace chose to peddle second-hand hallucinations. They were free to loot his alphas, if they cared to. So long as he got some decent entertainment for his piece and a half, his proprietary interests ended there.

He went under.

Abruptly he was Class Two, the occupant of a villa on an artificial island in the Mediterranean. Wearing nothing but a strip of green cloth about his waist, he lay restfully on a fat pneumochair at the edge of the sea. A girl paddled back and forth in the crystal water, her tanned skin gleaming when she broke the surface. She smiled at him. Pomrath acknowledged her with a negligent wave of his hand. She looked quite lovely in the water, he told himself.

He was viceroy for interpersonal relations in Moslem East, a nice soft Class Two sinecure that involved nothing more than an occasional visit to Mecca and a few conferences each winter in Cairo. He had a pleasant home near Fargo, North Dakota, and a decent apartment in the New York zone of Appalachia, and of course this island in the Mediterranean. He firmly expected to reach Class One in the next personnel kickover of the High Government. Danton consulted with him frequently. Kloofman had invited him to dinner several times down on Level One Hundred. They had discussed wines. Kloofman was something of a connoisseur; he and Pomrath had spent a splendid evening analyzing the virtues of a Chambertin that the synthesizers had produced back in '74. That was a good year, '74. Especially for the bigger Burgundies.

Helaine crawled up out of the water and stood incandescently bare before him, her tanned, full-blown body shimmering in the warm sunlight.

"Darling, why didn't you come swimming?" she asked.

"I was thinking. Very delicate plans."

"You know that that gives you a headache! Isn't there a government to do the thinking for you?"

"Underlings like your brother Joe? Don't be foolish, love. There's the government, and there's the High Government, and the two are quite distinct. I have my responsibilities. I have to sit here and think."

"What are you thinking about?"

"Helping Kloofman assassinate Danton."

"Really, love? But I thought you were in the Danton faction!"

Pomrath smiled. "I was. Kloofman, though, is a connoisseur of fine wines. He tempted me. Do you know what he's devised for Danton? It's magnificent. An autonomic laser programmed to put a beam through him at the exact moment when he—"

"Don't tell me," Helaine said. "I might give away the secret!" She turned, presenting her back to him. Pomrath let his eyes rove up and down the succulent voluptuousness of her. She had never looked more delightful, he thought. He wondered if he should participate in Kloofman's assassination scheme. Danton might reward him well for information. It was worth further thought.

The butler came rolling out of the villa and planted itself on four stubby telescoping legs beside Pomrath's lounge chair. Pomrath regarded the gray metal box with affection. What could be better than a homeostatic butler, programmed to its master's cycle of alcohol consumption?

"A filtered rum," Pomrath said.

He accepted the drink, which was extended toward him by a spidery arm of crosshatched titanium fibers. He sipped it. A hundred yards off shore, the sea abruptly began to bubble and boil, as though something monstrous were churning upward from the depths. A vast corkscrew-shaped nose broke the surface. A metal kraken, paying a visit. Pomrath gestured in the defense-motion, and instantly the guardian cells of the island threw up a picket fence of evenly spaced copper wire, each strand eight feet high and a sixteenth of an inch thick. The defense screen glowed between the strands.

The kraken lumbered toward the shore. It did not challenge the defensive screen. Rearing twenty feet out of the water, the bulky grayish-green object cast a long shadow across Pomrath and Helaine. It had large yellow eyes. A lid opened in the tubular skull, and a panel slid forward, out of which a human figure descended. So the kraken was merely a means of transportation, Pomrath observed. He recognized the figure who was coming ashore, and ordered the screen to drop.

It was Danton.

Cold eyes, sharply beaked nose, thin lips, swarthy skin betokening a more than usually mixed ancestry: Danton. As he stepped ashore, the Class One potentate nodded courteously to the nude Helaine and held both palms out to the apprehensive Pomrath. Pomrath tapped the butler's control panel; the metal box scuttled off to fetch a pneumochair for the newcomer. Danton settled into it. Pomrath procured a drink for him. Danton thanked him kindly. Helaine sprawled out on her belly to sunbathe.

Danton said quietly, "About Kloofman, now. The time has come—"

Pomrath woke, the taste of old rags in his mouth.

It was always like that, he thought sadly. Just as the hallucination got really exciting, the effect wore off. Now and then, experimentally, he had paid for a double-strength jolt so he could enjoy the fantasy longer. Even then, though, the mid-hallucination interruption was the rule. TO BE CONTINUED, the mask always said, ringing down the curtain. But what did he expect? A neatly rounded episode, beginning, middle, climax, resolution? Since when did the universe work that way? He elbowed up from the couch and headed back to the front desk to drop off the mask.

"You have a good one, Norm?" Jerry asked.

"Terrific," Pomrath said. "I was demoted to Class Twenty and put in maximum confinement. Then they found work for me as assistant to a sanitation robot. I was the one who worked the squeegee. After that I started to get cancer of the inner ear, and—"

"Hey, don't fool me. You got a dream like that here?"

"Sure," said Pomrath. "Not bad for a piece and a half, was it? Some fun!"

"You got a hell of a sense of humor, Norm. I don't know, a guy like you, where you think up the jokes."

Pomrath smiled thinly. "It's a gift from heaven. I don't question a thing like that. It comes to you out of the blue, like cancer of the inner ear. See you, Jerry."

He walked out and took the shaft to the top of the tank. It was late, close to dinnertime. He was in the mood for walking, but he knew Helaine would bend the walls if he dawdled like that on the way home, so he made for the nearest quickboat ramp. As he approached it, Pomrath saw a seedy figure coming toward him at a rapid clip. Pomrath tensed. I'm ready for anything, he thought. Just let him try some funny stuff.

"Read this," the man said, and jammed a crumpled minislip into Pomrath's hand.

Pomrath unfolded the tough, yellowish synthetic fiber. The message was simple, printed in purple letters right in the center of the slip:

OUT OF WORK?
SEE LANOY

That's interesting, Pomrath thought. I must have the look of the hard-core unemployed in my eyes, by now. Out of work? Sure!

But who the hell is this Lanoy?

five

Martin Koll made a great show of rearranging the papers on his desk, to cover a confusion that he was scarcely eager to let Quellen see. The CrimeSec had just brought Koll a very disturbing proposition, as full of ricocheting implications as an image trapped between two mirrors. Koll, in turn, would have to refer it to the High Government for a judgment. He would gladly have impaled Quellen on a rusty spike for having caused such trouble for him. Agreed, it was a clever proposal. But cleverness was out of character for Quellen. The man was dogged, methodical, reasonably adept, but that was no reason for him to present his superior with a treacherous proposition like this.

"Let me see if I grasp it," said Koll, who grasped it all too perfectly. "Your search of the hopper records has produced an authentic individual named Mortensen who is listed as having departed for the past from next month. It's your suggestion to monitor him, track him to his contact point, and if necessary prevent him forcibly from completing his trip to the past by arresting those who have agreed to send him there."

Quellen nodded. "That's it."

"You realize that it would be a direct interference with the past, in a deliberate way that's never been tried before, so far as I know?"

"I realize it," said Quellen. "That's why I came to you for authorization. I'm caught between two imperatives: catch the time-travel slyster, and preserve the orderly structure of history. Obviously this Mortensen is in contact with the slyster, or will be, if May 4 is his actual departure date. So if we slap a tracer on him—"

"Yes," Koll said drily. "You've said that already. I appreciate the difficulty."

"Do you have an instruction for me?"

Koll fidgeted with his papers again. He suspected that Quellen was doing this intentionally, putting his boss on the spot in a rare display of temperament. Koll was cognizant of the niceties of the situation. For ten years now he had made Quellen dance to *his* tune, compelling him to catch one hot assignment after another and then watching with some amusement as Quellen brought his limited capacities into play to deal with the problem. Koll admitted that there had been a element of sadism in his treatment of Quellen. It was fair enough; Koll was entitled to his personality faults, just like everyone else, and it seemed justifiable to him to release his aggressions through hostility toward the uncomplaining Quellen. All the same, it was a bother to have Quellen concoct a mess like this by way of revenge.

After a long moment of awkward silence Koll said, "I can't give you an instruction just yet. I'll have to consult with Spanner, of course. And most likely we'll need to get an advisory view from other quarters."

Meaning the High Government. Koll did not fail to observe the small smile of triumph that passed rapidly over Quellen's amiable features. Quellen was enjoying this, there could be no doubt of it.

"I'll hold off taking critical action until further word, sir," the CrimeSec said.

"You'd better," Koll replied.

Quellen went out. Koll dug his fingernails into his palms until his hands throbbed with pain. Then, with quick, disgusted taps of his fingers, he punched the autosec buttons until the machine disgorged a spool of his conversation with Quellen. That was for Spanner to study. And after that—

Spanner was out, just now. Checking on some complaint in another department. Koll, perspiring badly, wished that Quellen had waited until a time when Spanner was in the office before presenting this Mortensen nonsense. But no doubt that was part of Quellen's devilish plan, too. Koll bitterly resented being persecuted by the underling. He closed his eyes and saw Quellen's face on the inside of the lids: long straight nose, pale blue eyes, cleft chin. An ordinary face, a forgettable face. Some might even say a handsome face. No one had ever called Martin Koll handsome. On the other hand, he was clever. Far cleverer than the hapless Quellen, or so Koll had always thought, until this afternoon.

An hour later, Spanner came back. As he settled into his desk like a beast returning from a gorging meal, Koll slid the spool over to him.

"Play this. Then tell me what you think."

"Can't you give me a précis?"

"Play it. It's simpler," Koll said.

Spanner played it, mercifully using his earphone so Koll would not have to listen to the conversation again. When the spool had run its course, Spanner looked up. He tugged at the flesh of his throat and said, "It's a good chance to catch our man, isn't it?"

Koll closed his eyes. "Follow my train of thought. We tag Mortensen. He does not go back in time. He does not have the five children he is credited with fathering. Three of those five children, let us say, carry significant historical vectors. One of them grows up to be the father of the assassin of Secretary-General Tze. One of them becomes the grandfather of the unknown girl who carried the cholera to San Francisco. One of them is responsible for the line of descent that culminates in Flaming Bess. Now, since Mortensen never actually reaches his destination in the past, none of those three are born."

"Look at it another way," said Spanner. "Mortensen goes back and has five children. Two of them remain spinster girls. The third is killed falling through thin ice. The fourth becomes a common laborer and has some children who never amount to anything. The fifth—"

"How do you know," asked Koll quietly, "what the consequences of removing a single common laborer from the matrix of the past would be? How do you know what incalculable changes would be worked by removing even a spinster? *Do you want to risk it, Spanner?* Do you want the responsibility?"

"No."

"Neither do I. It's been possible to intercept hoppers for four years, now, simply by going through the records and catching them before they take off. No one's done it. No one's even suggested it, so far as I know, until the fiendish idea was hatched in the mind of our friend Quellen."

"I doubt that," said Spanner. "As a matter of fact, I've thought of it myself."

"And kept the idea to yourself."

"Well, yes. I hadn't had the time to work out the implications. But I'm sure it's occurred to others in the government who have been working on the hopper problem. Perhaps it's already been done, eh, Koll?"

"Very well," said Koll. "Call Quellen and ask him to file a formal request for approval of his plan. Then you sign it."

"No. We'll both sign it."

"I refuse to take the responsibility."

"In that case, so do I," Spanner said.

They smiled at each other in non-amusement. The obvious conclusion was all that was left.

"In that case," said Koll, "we must take it to Them for a decision."

"I agree. You handle it."

"Coward!" Koll snorted.

"Not really. Quellen brought the matter to you. You discussed it with me and got an advisory opinion that confirmed your own feelings. Now it's back to you, and you're the one who's riding it. Ride it right up to Them." Spanner smiled cordially. "You aren't afraid of Them, are you?"

Koll shifted uncomfortably in his seat. At his level of authority and responsibility, he had the right of access to the High Government. He had used it several times in the past, never with any degree of pleasure. Not *direct* access, of course; he had spoken face to face with a few Class Two people, but his only contacts with Class One had been on the screen. On one occasion Koll had spoken with Danton, and three times with Kloofman, but he had no way of being certain that the images on the screen were in fact those of authentic human beings. If something said it was Kloofman, and spoke in Kloofman's voice, and looked like the tridims of Kloofman that hung in public places, that still did not necessarily mean that there now was or ever had been such an actual person as Peter Kloofman.

"I'll call and see what happens," said Koll.

He did not want to make the call from his own desk. The need for physical motion was suddenly great in him. Koll rose, too abruptly, and scuttled out, down the hall, into a darkened communicator booth. The screen brightened as he keyed in the console.

One hardly dared to pick up the phone and call Kloofman, naturally. One went through channels. Koll's route to the top was through David Giacomin, Class Two, the viceroy for internal criminal affairs. Giacomin existed. Koll had seen him in the flesh, had touched his hand on one instance, had even spent a numbing two hours at Giacomin's private domain in East Africa, one of the most memorable and harrowing experiences in Koll's entire life.

He put through the call to Giacomin. In less than fifteen minutes the viceroy was on screen, smiling pleasantly at Koll with that easy benevolence that a Class Two man of secure ego could afford to display. Giacomin was a man of about fifty, Koll thought, with close-cropped iron-gray hair, lips that ran lopsidedly across his face, and a furrowed forehead. His left eye had been damaged irreparably some time in the past; in its place he wore a stubby fiber-receptor whose glass rods were plugged directly into his brain.

"What is it, Koll?" he asked amiably.

"Sir, one of my subordinates has proposed an unusual method of obtaining information about the hopper phenomenon. There's some controversy about whether we should proceed along the suggested path of action."

"Why don't you tell me all about it?" Giacomin said, his voice as warm and comforting as that of a frood begging to know about your most severe neurosis.

An hour later, toward the end of his working day, Quellen learned from Koll that nothing had been settled concerning Mortensen. Koll had talked to Spanner, and then he had talked to Giacomin, and now Giacomin was talking to Kloofman, and no doubt one of Them would be handing down The Word on the Mortensen project in a few days. Meanwhile, Quellen was to sit tight and take no provocative action. There was still plenty of time between now and Mortensen's documented May 4 departure date.

Quellen did not feel any sense of delight at the trouble he was causing. Tagging Mortensen was a clever idea, yes; but it was dangerous sometimes to be too clever. Quellen knew that he had made Koll uncomfortable. That never paid. For all he could tell, Koll had made Giacomin uncomfortable too, and now Giacomin was troubling

Kloofman, which meant that Quellen's clever proposal was stirring eddies of annoyance all the way to the very top of the global power structure. When Quellen had been younger and seething with ambitions to rise to Class Seven eminence, he would have liked nothing better than to win such attention to himself. Now, though, he *was* Class Seven, so he had attained the private apartment that was his dream, and further promotions would gain him little. Besides, his highly illegal nest in Africa weighed on his conscience. The last thing he wanted was to have a member of the High Government say, "This man Quellen is very clever—find out all you can about him." Quellen wished to remain inconspicuous, these days.

Still, he could not have let himself suppress the Mortensen idea. He had official responsibilities to fulfill, and the extent of his private deviation from the residence laws made him all the more conscientious about doing his public duties.

Before going home for the day, Quellen sent for Stanley Brogg.

The beefy assistant said at once, "We've got a wide net out for the slyster, CrimeSec. It's only a matter of days or even hours before we know his identity."

"Good," said Quellen. "I've got another line of approach for you to begin on. But this has to be handled with care, because it hasn't been officially approved yet. There's a man named Donald Mortensen planning to take his time-hop on May 4. Check him in the records you gave me; that's where I found out about him. I want tracers put on him. Check his activities and contacts. But it's got to be done with extreme delicacy. I can't stress that too highly, Brogg."

"All right. Mortensen."

"Delicately. If this man finds out we're tracing him, it could lead to a gigantic mess for all of us. Demotions or even worse. So get it straight: work around him, but don't even graze him. Otherwise it'll go hard for you."

Brogg smiled slyly. "You mean you'll drop me a couple of classes if I bungle?"

"Quite likely."

"I don't think you'd do that, CrimeSec. Not to *me*."

Quellen met the fat man's eyes steadily. Brogg was becoming offensive lately, taking too keen a relish in the power he held over Quellen. His accidental discovery of

54

Quellen's African villa was the great torment of the Crime-Sec's life.

"Get out of here," Quellen said. "And remember to be careful about Mortensen. It's very possible that this line of investigation will be quashed by the High Government, and if it is we'll all be frying if They find out we've alerted Mortensen."

"I understand," said Brogg. He left.

Quellen wondered if he should have done that. What if word came down via Giacomin that Mortensen was to be left alone? Well, Brogg was competent enough—too competent, sometimes. And there was really not much time to handle the Mortensen situation if approval did come through. Quellen had to initiate the project in advance. On a speculative basis, so to speak.

He had done all he could for now. Fleetingly he considered the idea of getting Brogg to handle the whole filthy case while he went back to Africa, but he decided that that would be inviting disaster. He shut up his office and went outside to catch the nearset quickboat back to his little Class Seven apartment. In the next few weeks, he knew, he might be able to slip off to Africa for an hour or two at a time, but no more than that. He was mired in Appalachia until the hopper crisis was over.

Returning to his apartment, Quellen discovered that he had neglected to keep his foodstocks in good supply. Since his stay in Appalachia threatened to be long or possibly permanent, he decided to replenish his stores. Sometimes Quellen ordered by phone, but not today. He fastened the *Privacy* radion to his door again and went down the twisting flyramp to the supply shop, intending to stock up for a long siege.

As he made his way down, he noticed a sallow-looking man in a loose-fitting purple tunic heading in the opposite direction up the ramp. Quellen did not recognize him, but that was unsurprising; in the crowded turmoil of Appalachia, one never got to know very many people, just a handful of neighbors and relatives, and a few service employees like the keeper of the local supply shop.

The sallow-looking man stared curiously at Quellen. He seemed to be saying something with his eyes. Quellen felt profoundly uncomfortable about the contact. In his departmental work, he had learned a good deal about the various classes of molesters one could encounter on the streets. The ordinary sexual kind, of course; but also the ones who sidled up to you and punctured your veins to inject the addictive dose of some infernal drug like helidone, or the sinister sorts given to jamming carcinogens against your skin in a crowd, or perhaps the secret agents who subtly stuck a molecular probe into your flesh that would transmit every word of your conversation to a distant pickup point. Such things happened all the time.

"Take it and read it," the sallow-faced man muttered.

He brushed against Quellen and shoved a wadded minislip into his hand. There was no way Quellen could have avoided the contact. The stranger could have done anything to him in that brief instant; right now Quellen's bone calcium might be turning to jelly, or his brain sloughing off through his nostrils, all to satisfy the gratuitous needs of some bump-killer. But it seemed that all the man had done was to put some kind of advertisement into Quellen's palm. Quellen unfolded the minislip after the other had disappeared up the flyramp, and read it:

OUT OF WORK?
SEE LANOY

That was all. Instantly Quellen's CrimeSec facet came into play. Like most lawbreakers in public office, he was vigorous in prosecution of other lawbreakers, and there was something in Lanoy's handbill that smacked of illegality, not just the offensive means of person-to-person transmission but also the offer itself. Was Lanoy running some kind of job placement operation? But that was a government responsibility! Quellen swung hastily around with the thought of pursuing the rapidly retreating sallow-faced man. He caught one last glimpse of the loose purple tunic, and then the man was gone. He could have gone almost anywhere after leaving the flyramp.

Out of work? See Lanoy.

Quellen wondered who Lanoy was and what his magic remedy might be. He made up his mind that he would have Leeward or Brogg look into the matter.

Carefully stowing the minislip in his pocket, Quellen entered the supply shop. The lead-lined door swung back to admit him. Robot merchandise-pickers were scuttling down the shelves, taking inventories, filling orders. The red-faced little man who ran the shop—as a front for the computers, naturally; what housewife wanted to gossip

56

with a computer?—greeted Quellen with an unusual display of heartiness.

"Oh, it's the CrimeSec! We haven't been honored by you in a long time, CrimeSec," the rotund shopkeeper said. "I was beginning to think you'd moved. But that's impossible, isn't it? You'd have notified me if you had gotten a promotion."

"Yes, Greevy, that's true. I've just not been around lately. Very busy these days. Investigations." Quellen frowned. He did not want the news of his frequent absences noised all around the community. Quickly, edgily, he grabbed up the greasy gray binding of the basic catalog and began to call off numbers. Canned foods, powdered concentrates, staples, all the components of a basic diet. He scrawled his list and jammed it before the sensors while the shopkeeper looked on benignly.

Greevy said, "Your sister was in yesterday."

"Helaine? I haven't seen much of her lately."

"She looks poorly, CrimeSec. Terribly thin. I programmed some Calfill for her, but she didn't want it. Has she been to the medics?"

"I really don't know," said Quellen. "Her husband's had some medical training. Not a doctor, just a technician, but if there's anything wrong with her he ought to be able to diagnose it. If he's got his wits still working. The rest of him certainly isn't."

"That's a trifle unfair, CrimeSec. I'm sure Mr. Pomrath would be happy to work more often. Why, I *know* it. No one likes to be idle. Your sister says he's really suffering. In fact—" the shopkeeper leaned close to whisper conspiratorially "—I shouldn't be telling you this, maybe, but there's some bitterness about you in that family. They think that perhaps, with your political influence—"

"I can't do a thing for them! Not a thing!" Quellen realized he was shouting. What business was it of this damned shopkeeper's that Norman Pomrath was out of work? How dare he meddle like this? Quellen struggled for calm. He found it, somehow, apologized for his outburst, quickly left the supply shop.

He stepped out into the street for a moment and stood watching as the multitudes streamed past. Their clothes were of all designs and colors. They talked incessantly. The world was a beehive, vastly overpopulated and getting more so daily, despite all the restrictions on childbirth. Quellen longed for the quiet retreat he had built at such

57

great cost and with so much trepidation. The more he saw of crocodiles, the less he cared for the company of the mobs who swarmed the crowded cities.

It was an orderly world, of course. Everybody numbered, labelled, registered, and tagged, not to say constantly monitored. How else could you govern a world of eleven or twelve or maybe thirty billion people without imposing a construct of order on them? Yet Quellen was in a fine position to know that within that superficial appearance of order, all sorts of shamelessly illegal things went on—not, as in Quellen's case, justifiable efforts to escape an intolerable existence, but shady, vicious, unpardonable things. Take the drug addictions, he thought. There were laboratories in five continents grinding out new drugs as fast as the old addictions were abolished. Right now they were pushing some kind of deathly alkaloids, and they pushed them in the most flagrant ways. A man walks into a sniffer palace hoping to buy half an hour of innocent hallucinatory amusement, and buys a hellish addiction instead. Or, aboard a quickboat, a man's hand traverses a woman's body in what seems like something no more deplorable than an indecent caress, but two days later the woman discovers she has developed an addiction, and must seek medical help to find out what it is she's addicted to.

Things like that, thought Quellen. Ugly, inhuman things. We are a dehumanized people. We injure one another without any need but the simple need to do injury. And when we turn to each other for help, we get no response but fear and withdrawal. Stay away, stay away! Let me alone!

And consider this Lanoy, Quellen ruminated, fingering the minislip in his pocket. Some kind of crookedness going on there, yet it was concealed well enough to have avoided the attention of the Secretariat of Crime. What did the computer files say about Lanoy? How did this Lanoy manage to hide his illegal activities from his family or roommates? Surely he did not live alone. Such an outlaw could not be Class Seven. Lanoy must be some shrewd prolet, running a free-enterprise swindle for his own private benefit.

Quellen felt a strange kinship with the unknown Lanoy, much as it repelled him to admit it. Lanoy, too, was beating the game. He was a wily one, possibly worth knowing. Quellen frowned. Quickly he moved on, back to his apartment.

six

Peter Kloofman lay sprawled out in a huge tube of nutrient fluid while the technicians changed his left lung. His chest panel was wide open on its hinges, exactly as though Kloofman were some sort of robot undergoing repair. He was no robot. He was mere mortal flesh and blood, but not very mortal. At the age of a hundred thirty-two, Kloofman had undergone organ replacements so frequently that there was very little left of his original persona except for the gray slab of his wily brain itself, and even that was no stranger to the surgeon's beam. Kloofman was willing to submit to such things gladly, for the sake of preserving his existence, which is to say his infinite power. He was real. Danton was not. Kloofman preferred to keep things that way.

"David Giacomin is here to see you," purred a voice from the probe rivited just within his skull.

"Admit him," said Kloofman.

Some twenty years ago he had had himself reconstructed so that he could carry on the business of the state even while undergoing regenerative surgery. It would have been impossible to remain in power, otherwise. Kloofman was the only flesh-and-blood member of Class One, which meant that all power lines converged toward him. He delegated as much as he could to the assortment of cams and relays that went by the name of Benjamin Danton; but Danton, after all, was unreal, and in the long run even he was only an extension of the tireless Kloofman. It had not always been this way. Before the Flaming Bess affair there had been three members of Class One, and still further back Kloofman had been but one of five.

He carried on satisfactorily this way, however. And there was no reason why he could not continue to bear his unique burden for another six or seven hundred years. No man in all the history of the world had held the power Peter Kloofman held. In his occasional moments of fatigue he found that a comforting thing upon which to reflect.

Giacomin entered. He stood in a position of relaxed attentiveness beside the nutrient tub in which Kloofman lay. Kloofman valued Giacomin highly. He was one of perhaps two hundred Class Two individuals who provided the indispensable underpinning for the High Government. Between Class Two and Class Three was a qualitative gulf. Class Two understood the way the world was run; Class Three, on the other hand, enjoyed great comforts, but no true understanding. To a Class Three surgeon or administrator, Danton was probably real, and other unnamed Class Ones existed as well. Giacomin, privy to the knowledge a Class Two man had, was aware of the truth.

"Well?" Kloofman asked, watching with detached interest as the surgeons lifted the gray, foamy mass of the replacement lung and inserted it in his gaping chest cavity "What's the story for today, David?"

"Hoppers."

"Have they located the process yet?"

"Not yet," said Giacomin. "They're taking steps, though. It won't be long."

"Good, good," murmured Kloofman. This enterprise of illicit time travel troubled him more than he cared to admit. For one thing, it went on despite the best efforts of the government to track it to its source, and that was bothersome. But of course it was only a few days since Kloofman had requested a detect on the operation, anyway. Much more annoying was the fact that for all his power he could not reach out instantly, seize this temporal process, and put it to his own uses. It had been developed independently of the instrumentalities of the High Government. Thus it was a conspicuous reminder to Kloofman that not even he was omnipotent.

Giacomin said, "There's a problem. They've thought of isolating a potential hopper and keeping him from making the jump."

Kloofman moved convulsively in his bath. Fluid splashed into his chest cavity. Hemeostatic pumps imperturbably removed it, and a surgeon clamped his lips together and went about the job of stapling the new lung in place without comment. The world leader said, "A listed hopper? One who's been recorded?"

"Yes."

"Have you permitted this?"

"I brought it to you. I've got a hold on it until The Word comes down."

"Kill it," said Kloofman decisively. "Beyond a doubt. I go further: make absolutely certain that there's no interference with any listed hoppers. Take that as a flat rule. Anyone who has left must leave. Yes? That's The Word, David. It goes out to all departments that are even remotely connected with the hopper business."

As he spoke, Kloofman felt a faint stinging sensation in the fleshy part of his left thigh. Sedation; he must be getting too excited. The automatic monitoring system was compensating by chemical means, dilating arteries, flooding his system with useful enzymes. He could do better than that. Consciously, he willed himself to be calm even in the face of this threat. Giacomin looked concerned.

Kloofman grew tranquil. Giacomin said, "That was all I wanted to report. I'll pass your instructions along."

"Yes. And notify the Danton programmers. Anything going through his office should carry the same notification. This is something too important to let slide. I don't understand how I failed to anticipate the possibility."

Giacomin departed, making his way carefully around the tank and out of the faintly clammy atmosphere of the chamber. Kloofman eyed the green vitreous walls with displeasure. He realized that he should have been forewarned. It was the job of those in Class Two to plot the pitfalls for him in advance, and they had been cognizant of the hopper problem for some time now. As far back as '83, contingency schedules had been drawn to deal with the hopper problem. Why had they not included *this*? Of all things to forget!

Kloofman forgave himself for overlooking it. The others, though—they were in for a declassing.

Out loud he said, "Imagine what could have happened if anybody had begun meddling with the registered and documented hoppers. Pulling chunks out of the past— why, it might have turned the world upside-down!"

The surgeons did not reply. It would be worth their classifications if they ever spoke to Kloofman except on matters of their own sphere of professional competence.

61

They closed his chest and ran anemostats over it. The instant healing process began. The temperature in the nutrient bath began to descend as the automatic regulators prepared Kloofman for his return to independent motility.

He was badly shaken, not by postoperative shock—that was unknown these days—but by the implications of what had almost happened. Meddling with the past! Pulling hoppers from the matrix! Suppose, he thought fretfully, some bureaucrat in Class Seven or Nine or thereabouts had gone ahead on his own authority, trying to win a quick uptwitch by dynamic action, and had rounded up a few known hoppers in advance of their departure. Thereby completely snarling the fabric of the time-line and irrevocably altering the past.

Everything might have been different, Kloofman thought.

I might have become a janitor, a technician, a peddler of fever pills. I might never have been born. Or I might have landed in Class Seven with Danton real and in charge. Or there might have been total anarchy, no High Government whatsoever. Anything. Anything. A wholly different world. The transformation would have come like a thief in the night, and the editing of the past would naturally be indetectable, so that I would never know there had been a change in my status. Perhaps there had already been several changes. Kloofman thought suddenly.

Was it possible?

Had two or three hoppers already been thwarted in their documented escapes by some zealous official? And had fundamental changes in the historical patterns of the past five centuries resulted, changes that could never be observed? Kloofman felt an abrupt and fatiguing sense of the instability of the universe. Here he was, two thousand feet down in the solid earth, living as always at the bottom of civilization, for the High Government was the lowest level occupied, and he had known absolute power for decades of a kind never remotely comprehended by Attila or Genghis Khan or Napoleon or Hitler, and yet he could feel the roots of the past ripping loose like torn strings about him. It sickened him. Some faceless individual, a mere government man, could wreck everything in a harmless blunder, and there was nothing Kloofman could do to prevent it from happening. It might already have begun to happen.

I should never have embarked on this hopper enterprise Kloofman thought.

But that was wrongheaded, he knew. He had done the right thing, but he had done it carelessly, without full consideration of the danger factors. Before turning his bureaucracy loose on catching the shipper of time-hoppers, he should have issued strict orders concerning interference with the past. He trembled at the thought of the vulnerability he had opened for himself. At any time since 2486, his entire edifice of power, so laboriously constructed over so many years, could have been wrecked by the blind whim of an underling.

The stabs of a dozen homeostatic injections reminded Kloofman that he was losing his calmness again.

"Get me Giacomin," he said.

The viceroy entered a few moments later, looking puzzled at the peremptory recall. Kloofman leaned heavily forward, straining himself half out of the tank, causing the servomechanisms within his body to whine in tinny protest. "I just wanted to make certain," he said, "that there was full understanding of my instruction. *No* interference with hopper departures. None. None whatever. Clear?"

"Of course."

"Do I worry you, David? Do you think I'm a garrulous old man who ought to have his brain scraped? Let me tell you why I worry about this thing. I control the present and to some extent the future, right? Right. But not the past. How can I control the past? I see a whole segment of time that's beyond my authority. I admit to being frightened. Maintain my authority over the past, David. See that it remains inviolate. What has happened must happen."

"I've already taken steps to see that it will," said Giacomin.

Kloofman dismissed him a second time, feeling reassured but not sufficiently so. He summoned Mauberley, the Class Two man in charge of running the Danton operation. As one who considered himself a quasi-immortal, Kloofman did not spend much time designating heirs apparent, but he had high respect for Mauberley, and regarded his as a possible eventual successor. Mauberley entered. He was sixty years old, vigorous and muscular, with a flat-featured face and wiry, thick hair. Kloofman briefed him on the new development. "Giacomin is already at work on the problem," he said. "You work on it too. Redundancy, that's the secret of effective government. Get Danton to make an official proclamation. Circulate it downward through Class Seven. This is an emergency!"

Mauberley said, "Do you believe there have already been changes in the past as a result of contra-hopper activity?"

"No. But there could be. We'd never know."

"I'll deal with it," he said, and left.

Kloofman rested. After a while, he had himself withdrawn from his nutrient bath and taken to his office. He had not been to the surface in sixteen years. The upper world had become slightly unreal to him; but he saw no harm in that, since he was well aware that to most of the inhabitants of the upper world *he* was slightly unreal, or more than slightly. Reciprocity, he thought. The secret of effective government. Kloofman lived in a complex of interlocking tunnels spreading out for hundreds of miles. At any given time, machines with glittering claws were energetically at work extending his domain. He hoped to have the world girdled with a continuous network of High Government access routes in another ten years or so. His personal Midgard Serpent of transportation. Strictly speaking, there was no need for it; he could govern just as effectively from a single room as from any point along a world-rimming tunnel. But he had his whims. What was the use of being the supreme leader of the entire world, Kloofman wondered, if he could not occasionally indulge a small whim?

He moved on purring rollers to the master control room and allowed his attendants to attach him to contact leads. It bored him to depend on words for his knowledge of external events. One of the many surgical reconstructs that had been performed on him over the years allowed a direct neural cut-in; Kloofman could and did enter directly into the data stream, becoming a relay facet of the computer web itself. Then, only then, did a kind of ecstasy overwhelm him.

He nodded, and the flow of data began.

Facts. Births and deaths, disease statistics, transportation correlations, power levels, crime rates. Synapse after synapse clenched tight as Kloofman absorbed it all. Far above him, billions of people went through their daily routines, and he entered in some way into the life of each of them, and they entered into his. His perceptions were limited, of course. He could not detect individual fluctuations in the data except as momentary surges. Yet he could extrapolate them. At this very instant, he knew, a hopper was departing for the past. A life subtracted from the present. What about mass? Was it conserved? The data on planetary mass failed to take into account the possibility of a sudden and total subtraction. Two hundred pounds abruptly removed from now and thrust into yesterday—how could it be possible, Kloofman wondered? It was done, though. The records showed it. Thousands of hoppers thrust out of his time and into the time of his predecessors. How? How?

Peter Kloofman brushed the thought from his throbbing mind. It was an irrelevancy. What was relevant was the sudden, unthinkable possibility that the past might be altered, that all this might be taken away from him in a random fluctuation against which no defense existed. That struck horror into him. He filled his brain with data to drown out the possibility of total loss. He felt the onset of his delight.

Caesar, did you ever have the whole world running through your brain at once?

Napoleon, could you so much as imagine what it might be like to be plugged right into the master computers?

Sardanapalus, were there joys like this in Nineveh?

Kloofman's bulky body quivered. The mesh of fine capillary wires just beneath his skin glowed. He ceased to be Peter Kloofman, world leader, lone human member of Class One, benevolent despot, sublime planner, the accidental inheritor of the ages. Now he was everyone who existed. A flux of cosmic power surged in him. This was the true Nirvana! This was the ultimate Oneness! This was the moment of full rapture!

At such a time, it was not possible to brood on how easily it could all be taken away from him.

seven

Helaine Pomrath said, "Norm, who's Lanoy?"

"Who?"

"Lanoy. L—A—N—"

"Where did you hear that name?"

She showed him the minislip and watched his face carefully .His eyes flickered. He was off balance.

"I found this in your tunic last night," she said. " 'Out of work, see Lanoy,' it says. I just wondered who he was, what he could do for you."

"He—uh—runs some kind of employment bureau, I think. I'm not sure." Pomrath looked thoroughly uncomfortable. "Somebody slipped that to me as I was coming out of the sniffer palace."

"What good is it, if there's no address on it?"

"I guess you're supposed to follow it up," Pomrath said. "Hunt around, do some detective work. I don't know. Actually, I had forgotten all about it, to tell me the truth. Give it here."

She surrendered it. He took it quickly, and thrust it into his pocket. Helaine did not like the speed with which he got the incriminating document out of sight. Although she hadn't even a remote notion of its implications, she was easily able to detect her husband's guilt and general embarrassment.

Maybe he's planning a surprise for me, she thought. Maybe he's already been to this Lanoy and done something about getting a job, but he was saving it to tell me next week when it's our anniversary. And I bungled it by asking him questions. I should have let it go a while.

Her son Joseph, stark naked, stepped down from the

66

platform of the molecular bath. His sister, equally naked, got under it. Helaine busied herself with programming breakfast. Joseph said, "We're going to learn geography in school today."

"How lovely," Helaine said vaguely.

"Where's Africa?" the boy asked.

"Far away. Across the ocean somewhere."

"Can I go to Africa when I grow up?" Joseph persisted.

There was a shrill giggle from the bath. Marina whirled around and said, "Africa's where the Class Twos live! Are you going to be Class Two, Jo-Jo?"

The boy glowered at his sister. "Maybe. Maybe I'll be Class One. How do you know? *You* won't be anything. I got something you don't have already."

Marina made a face at him. All the same, she turned around to hide her undeveloped nine-year-old body from his beady eyes. From his corner of the room, Pomrath looked up from the morning faxtape and grunted, "Cut that out, both of you! Jo-Jo, get dressed! Marina, finish your bath!"

"I just said I wanted to go to Africa," the boy muttered.

"Don't speak back to your father," said Helaine. "Breakfast's ready, anyhow. Get dressed."

She sighed. Her head felt as though someone had poured powdered glass into it. The children always bickering, Norm sitting in the corner like a guest at his own wake, mysterious minislips popping up in the wash, four windowless walls hemming her in—no, it was too much. She didn't understand how she could tolerate it. Eat, sleep, bathe, make love, all in one little room. Thousands of grubby neighbors mired in the same bog. Picnic once a year, via stat to some faraway place that wasn't all built up yet—bread and circuses, keep the prolets happy. But it hurt to see a tree and then come back to Appalachia. There was actual pain in it, Helaine thought miserably. She had not bargained for this when she married Norm Pomrath. He had been full of plans.

The children ate and left for school. Norm remained where he was, turning and twisting the faxtape in his stubby fingers. Now and then he shared an item of news with her. "Danton's dedicating a new hospital in Pacifica next Tuesday. Totally automated, one big homeostat and no technicians at all. Isn't that nice? It reduces government expenditures when no employees are required. And here's a good one, too. Effective the first of May, oxy quotas in all commercial buildings are reduced by ten per cent. They say it's to enable additional gas supplies to reach householders. You remember that, Helaine, when they cut the home quota too around August. It always goes down. When it gets to the point where they're rationing air—"

"Norm, don't get worked up."

He ignored her. "How did all this happen to us? We've got a right to something better. Four million people per square inch, that's where we're heading. Build the houses a thousand stories high so there's room for everyone, and it takes a month to get down to street level or up to the quickboat ramp, but what of it? It's progress. And—"

"Do you think you'll be able to locate this Lanoy and get a job through him?" she asked.

"What we need," he went on, "is a first-class bacterial plague. Selective, of course. Wipe out all those who are lacking in functional job skills. That cuts the dole roll by a few billion units a day. Devote the tax money to makework programs for the rest. If that doesn't work, start a war. Extraterrestrial enemies, the Crab People from the Crab Nebula, everything for patriotism. Start a *losing* war. Cannonfodder."

He's cracking up, Helaine thought as her husband went on talking. It was an endless monologue these days, a spewing fountain of bitterness. She tried not to listen. Since he showed no sign of leaving the apartment, she did. She hurled the dishes into the disposal unit and said to him, "I'm going to visit the neighbors," and walked out just as he launched into an exposition of the virtues of controlled nuclear warfare as a means of population check. Random spasms of noise, that was what Norm Pomrath was producing these days. He had to hear himself talk, so that he did not forget he was still there.

Where shall I go, Helaine wondered?

Beth Wisnack, widowed by her time-hopping husband, looked smaller, grayer, sadder today than she had looked on Helaine's last visit. Beth's mouth was tightly drawn back in the quirk of suppressed rage. Behind the look of feminine resignation that she wore was inward fury: *how dare he do this to me, how could he abandon me like this?*

Courteously Beth offered an alcohol tube to her guest. Helaine smiled pleasantly, took the snub-ended red plastic

68

tube, thrust it against the fleshy part of her arm. Beth did the same. The ultrasonic snouts whirred; the stimulant spurted into their bloodstreams. An easy drunk, for those who did not like the taste of modern liquors. Helaine flickered her eyes, relaxing. She listened for a while to Beth's song of complaint, pitched all on one note.

Then Helaine said, "Beth, do you know about someone called Lanoy?"

Beth was at instant attention. "Who Lanoy? What Lanoy? Where did you hear of him? What do you know of him?"

"Not much. That's why I asked you."

"I heard the name, yes." Her pale eyes were agitated. "Bud mentioned it. I heard him talking, telling some other man, Lanoy this, Lanoy that ... It was the week before he ran out on me. Lanoy, he said. Lanoy will fix it."

Helaine reached for a second alcohol tube without waiting to be invited. There was a sudden chill inside her that needed to be thawed.

"Lanoy will fix what?" she asked.

Beth Wisnack subsided defeatedly. "I don't know. Bud never discussed things with me. But I heard him talking about this Lanoy, anyway. A lot of whispering going on. Just before he left, he was talking Lanoy all the time. I've got a theory about Lanoy. You want to hear?"

"Of course!"

Smiling, Beth said, "I think Lanoy's the one who runs the hopper business."

Helaine had thought so too. But she had come here to learn otherwise, not to have her worst fears confirmed. Tense, her hands trembling a little, she smoothed her tunic, shifted her position, and said, "You really think so?

"Bud talked Lanoy all week. Then he disappeared. He was hatching something and it had to do with Lanoy. I should know what? But I've got my theories. Bud met this Lanoy somewhere. They struck a deal. And—and—" The pain and rage welled too close to the surface. "And Bud left," Beth Wisnack said breathily. She popped another tube. Then she said, "Why do you ask?"

"I found a slip in Norman's clothes," Helaine said. "It was some kind of advert. *'Out of work? See Lanoy.'* I asked him about it. He got very embarrassed. Took the slip away from me, tried to tell me it was an employment agency, something like that. I could see he was lying. Hiding something. The trouble is, I don't know what."

"You better start worrying hard, Helaine."

"You think it's bad?"

"I think it's just the same as with Bud. Norm's in contact with them. He's probably trying to raise the money now. And they send him out. *Poof!* Gone. No husband. The widow Pomrath. Two kids, shift for yourself." Beth Wisnack's eyes were glittering strangely now. She did not look unhappy at the prospect that Helaine's husband might go hopper. It was the misery that craves company, Helaine knew. Let every husband in the world vanish into the maw of the past and perhaps Beth Wisnack would feel some delight.

Helaine fought to stay calm.

"When the police investigated Bud's disappearance," she said, "did you mention this person Lanoy to them?"

"I named him, yes. They wanted to know if Bud had been seeing anyone unusual just before he vanished, and I said I didn't know, but there was this name he had mentioned a few times, Lanoy, that I didn't know. They took it down. I don't know what they did about it. It isn't going to bring Bud back. You can only go one direction in time, you know. Backward. They don't have any machines back there to send people ahead again, and in any case I understand it isn't possible. You go back, you're stranded there for keeps. So when Norm goes—"

"He's not going," said Helaine.

"He's seeing Lanoy, isn't he?" Beth asked.

"All he had was the minislip. It didn't even have an address on it. He said he didn't know where to find Lanoy. And we aren't sure that Lanoy is connected with the hopper business, anyhow."

Beth's eyes sparkled. "The Lanoy mob is in contact with him," she said. "That means they can reach him any time. So he can reach them. And they'll send him back. He's going to be a hopper, Helaine. He's going to go."

Q.E.D.

A quickboat took her to the flamboyant skyscraper that housed the Secretariat of Crime. Some persistent work at the front desk yielded Helaine the information that her brother was at the office today, and if she cared to wait a while perhaps he would see her. She requisitioned an appointment with him. The machine asked for her thumbprint, and she gave it, and then sat down to wait in an anteroom draped with somber purplish fabrics.

Helaine was not accustomed to venturing out into the world of office buildings and walking servomechanisms. She stayed close to home, and did her shopping by remote contact. "Downtown"—the world at the end of the quick-boat routes—was a frightening place to her. She forced herself to remain cool. On a matter as serious as this, she had to see her brother face to face across a desk, so that he could not escape from her at the flick of a switch. She was terrified.

"The CrimeSec will see you," a flat impersonal vocoder voice told her.

She was ushered into the presence of her brother. Quellen stood up, flashed a quick, uncomfortable smile, beckoned her into a chair. The chair grabbed her and began to knead the muscles of her back. Helaine shuddered at the sensation, and pulled away in alarm as the invisible hands within the chair started to go to work on her thighs and buttocks. The delicate feedback sensors of the chair caught her mood, and the attentions ceased.

She looked uncertainly at her brother. Quellen seemed to be as ill at ease with her as she was with him; he tugged at his ear, clenched his jaws, popped his knuckles. They were practically strangers. They met on family occasions, but there had been no real communication between them for a long time. He was a few years older than she was. Once, they had been quite close, two devoted siblings bantering and heckling one another just as her Joseph and Marina did today. Helaine could remember her brother as a boy, stealing his peeks at her body in their one-room apartment, pulling her hair, helping her with her homework. Then he had begun his training for government service, and after that he had not been part of her world in any meaningful way. Now she was an edgy housewife and he was a busy public officer, and she was somewhat afraid of him.

For perhaps three minutes they exchanged friendly pleasantries about domestic matters. Helaine talked about her children, her social conscience unit in the apartment, her personal reading program. Quellen said very little. He was a bachelor, which set him further apart from her. Helaine knew that her brother kept company with some woman, somebody named Judith, but he rarely talked about her and seemed hardly ever even to think of her. There were times when Helaine suspected that Judith did not exist—that Quellen had invented her as camouflage for some solitary vice he preferred, or, worse, for some homosexual involvement. Sodomy was acceptable socially these days; it helped to keep the birth rate low. But Helaine did not like to think of her brother Joe taking part in such practices.

She brought the chatter to a deliberate end by asking about Judith. "Is she well? You've never kept your promise to bring her to visit us, Joe."

Quellen looked as uncomfortable at the mention of Judith as Norm Pomrath had looked while Helaine was questioning him about the Lanoy minislip. He said evasively, "I've mentioned the idea to her. She thinks it would be fine to meet you and Norm, but not just yet. Judith's a little disturbed by having to meet your children. Children unsettle her. But I'm sure we'll work something out." He flashed the quick, hollow smile again. Then he dismissed the touchy subject of Judith by getting down to the business at hand. "I'm sure this wasn't just a social call, Helaine."

"No. It's business, Joe. I see by the faxtapes that you're conducting an investigation of the hoppers."

"Yes. True."

"Norm's going to hop."

Quellen sat stiffly upright, his left shoulder rising higher than the right one. "What gives you that idea? Has he told you so himself?"

"No, of course not. But I suspect it. He's been very depressed lately, about not working and all that."

"Nothing new with him."

"More so than usual. You should hear the way he talks. He's so bitter, Joe! He talks absolute nonsense, just a stream of angry words that don't make any sense. I wish I could quote him for you. He's building up to some kind of psychological explosion, I know it. I can feel the steam gathering inside him." She winced. The chair was starting to massage her again. "He hasn't worked for months now, Joe."

Quellen said, "I'm aware of that. You know, the High Government is furthering a whole sequence of plans designed to alleviate the unemployment problem."

"That's fine. But in the meanwhile Norm isn't working, and I don't think it'll matter much longer. He's in contact with the hopper people and he's going to hop. Even while I'm sitting here telling you this, he might be getting into the machine!"

Her voice had risen to a tinny screech. She could hear the echoes of it go bouncing around in her brother's office. It seemed to her that the ends of her nerves had burst through her skin all over her body, and were jutting out like quills.

Quellen's manner changed. He seemed to make a conscious effort to relax, and he leaned forward benevolently, giving her a froodlike smile. Helaine expected him to ask, "Shall we now attempt to get to the bottom of this delusion of yours?" What he actually said, in honeyed, humoring tones, was, "Maybe you're getting overwrought for no real reason, Helaine. What makes you think he's having dealings with the hopper criminals?"

She told him about the Lanoy minislip, and about Norm's exaggerated reaction of unconcern when she had queried him on Lanoy. As she quoted the five-word slogan on the slip, Helaine was startled to see her brother's beaming look of phony solicitude give way for a moment to a blank expression betokening some sudden absolute terror within. Then Quellen recovered; but he had already betrayed himself. Helaine was sharp to detect such momentary flickers of the inner persona.

She said, "You know about Lanoy?"

"It happens that I've seen one of those slips, Helaine. They're being circulated pretty widely. You go up a quick-boat ramp and somebody comes up to you and hands one out. No doubt that's how Norm got his."

"And it's advertising for the hopper people, isn't it?"

"I've got no reason to think so," Quellen drawled, his eyes proclaiming his lie to her.

"Are you investigating Lanoy, though? I mean, if there's reason to suspect—"

"We're investigating, yes. And I repeat, Helaine, there's no necessary cause to feel that this person Lanoy is in any way connected with the hopper problem."

"But Beth Wisnack said that her husband Bud talked about Lanoy all week before he went."

"Who?"

"Wisnack. A recent hopper. When I asked her about Lanoy, Beth told me point-blank that he was responsible for Bud's disappearance, and she also said that it was a sure thing that Norm would be going too." Agitated, Helaine crossed and uncrossed her legs. The chair's dull brain picked up the evidence of her restlessness, and after

73

having been quiescent for a few minutes began to fondle her again.

Quellen said, "We can check this business of Norm's going hopper very easily." He swung around and produced a spool. "I have here the complete listing of all the documented hoppers who were recorded as they arrived in the past. This list was compiled recently for me and of course I haven't studied it completely, because it contains hundreds of thousands of names. But if Norm did hop, we'll find him here."

He activated the spool and began to search it, explaining in a half-mumble that the listings were alphabetical. Helaine sat rigidly as the search continued through the alphabet at a rate of thousands of bits per second. It would not take long for Quellen to reach the "P" entries. And then—

If Norm had gone, he would be entered here. His fate would be plain for her to see—his fate and hers, inscribed in this Doomsday Book of thermoplastic tape. She would learn that her marriage had been doomed three hundred years before she contracted it. She would find that her husband's name had been inscribed centuries ago on a roster of fugitives from this century. Why had that roster not been a matter of public record all this time? Because, she knew, it would lie like a dead hand across the soul of those who had hopped, would hop, must hop. What would it be like to grow up under the shadow of the knowledge that you were destined to leap from your own era?

"You see?" Quellen said triumphantly. "He isn't on the list."

"Does that mean he didn't hop?"

"I'd say so."

"But how can you be sure that all the hoppers are really listed?" Helaine demanded. "What if a lot of them slipped through?"

"It's possible."

"And the names," she went on. "If Norm gave a different name when he got to the past, he wouldn't be on your list either. Right?

Quellen looked glum. "There's always the possibility that he adopted a pseudonym," he admitted.

"You're hedging, Joe. You can't be sure he didn't hop. Even with the list."

"So what do you want me to do, Helaine?"

She took a deep breath. "You could arrest Lanoy before he sends Norm back in time."

"I've got to find Lanoy," Quellen observed. "And then I've got to have some proof that he's involved. So far there isn't even any circumstantial evidence, just a lot of conclusion-jumping on your part."

"Then arrest Norm."

"What?"

"Find him guilty of something and lock him up. Give him a year or two of corrective therapy. That'll keep him out of circulation until the hopper crisis is over. Call it protective custody."

"Helaine, I can't use the law as a private plaything for members of my family!"

"He's my husband, Joe. I want to keep him. If he goes back in time, I've lost him forever." Helaine stood up. She swayed, and had to grip Quellen's desk. How could she make him understand that she stood at the edge of an abyss? To hop was effectively the same as to die. She was fighting to keep her husband. And there sat her brother in the cloak of his righteousness, doing nothing while precious seconds ticked away.

"I'll do what I can," Quellen promised. "I'll look into this Lanoy. If you'd like to send Norm here, I'll talk to him and try to find out what's on his mind. Yes. Perhaps that's best. Get him to come to see me."

"If he's planning to hop," said Helaine, "he's not likely to tell you about it. He won't come within five miles of this building."

"Why don't you tell him that I want to talk to him about a job opportunity? He's been complaining that I haven't been doing anything for him, yes? All right. He'll come to me, thinking that I've got an opening for him. And I'll pump him about hopping. Subtly. If he knows anything, I'll get it out of him. We'll smash the hopper ring and there'll be no danger of his taking off. How does that sound, Helaine?"

"Encouraging. I'll talk to him. I'll send him to you. If he hasn't already taken off."

She moved toward the door. Her brother smiled once again. Helaine winced. She was fearful that Norm had already vanished irretrievably, while she sat here talking. She had to get back to him in a hurry. Until this crisis was over, she knew she must keep close watch.

"Remember me to Judith," Helaine said, and went out.

eight

Quellen had not enjoyed the interview with his sister. Helaine always left him feeling flayed. She was so visibly unhappy that it pained him to see her at all. Now she looked five or six years older than he was. He remembered Helaine at thirteen or so, virginal and radiant, naive enough to think that life held something wonderful for her. Here she was a few years short of forty, marooned within four walls, clawing like a demon to hang on to her morose, embittered husband, because he was just about all that she had.

Still, she had given him some useful information. Lanoy had been on Quellen's mind ever since the sallow-faced stranger had pressed the wadded minislip into his hand on the flyramp. The next day, Quellen had initiated a routine check, but it had turned up nothing tangible. A mere last name was useless to the computer. There were thousands of Lanoys in the world, and Quellen could scarcely investigate every one of them for possible criminal activities. A random scoop had yielded no information. Now, though, came Helaine with her intuitive conviction that Lanoy was behind the hopper business. And this woman she had mentioned, this Beth Wisnack—Quellen made a note to send a man around to talk to her again. No doubt Beth Wisnack had already been interrogated about her husband's disappearance, but she would have to be approached from the direction of Lanoy information this time.

Quellen considered the possibility of posting a guard on Norm Pomrath to prevent any untimely departure. He had been ordered in no ambiguous terms to leave Donald

Mortensen alone and to do no meddling with any of the listed hoppers. Koll had received The Word from Giacomin, who had it from the lips of Kloofman himself: "Hands off Mortensen."

They were afraid of changing the past. Quellen could feel the fear in them running right up to the High Government. It was within his power to shake the underpinnings of the universe. Pick up Donald Mortensen for questioning and put a laser bolt through his skull, for example.

"Sorry. Resisted arrest and had to be destroyed."

Yes. And then Donald Mortensen would never take off for the past on May 4. Which would upset the entire structure of the last few centuries. At the moment I shoot Mortensen, Quellen thought, everything will shift and it will turn out that we were conquered by an army of slimy centipedes from the Magellanic Clouds in A.D. 2257—a conquest that would have been prevented by one of the descendants of Donald Mortensen, if I hadn't been so thoughtless as to shoot him down.

Quellen had no intention of inviting the wrath of the High Government by interfering with the departure of Donald Mortensen. But Norm Pomrath was not on the hopper list. Was he covered by Kloofman's directive, then? Was Quellen required to abstain from any action that could possibly lead to the time-departure of any person whatever?

That made no sense. Therefore Quellen agreed with himself that he could without compromising himself keep watch on his brother-in-law and take steps to prevent Norm from going hopper. That would make Helaine happy. It might also, Quellen thought, contribute to an ultimate solution to this entire worrisome assignment.

"Get me Brogg," he said into his communicator mouthpiece.

Brogg turned out to be conducting an investigation outside the building. The other UnderSec, Leeward, entered Quellen's office.

The CrimeSec said, "I've got a possible lead. My brother-in-law Norm Pomrath is allegedly on the verge of seeking out a contact who'll help him become a hopper. I'm not sure there's any truth in it, but I want it checked. Slap an Ear on Pomrath and have him monitored on a twenty-four-hour, round-the-clock basis. If he utters so much as a syllable about hopping, we'll make our move."

"Yes, sir," said Leeward stolidly.

"There's also this matter of a certain Lanoy. Did anything new turn up?"

"Not yet, sir."

"I've learned that Pomrath's supposed contact man is this Lanoy. So that's our key syllable. Make sure that the monitors are triggered to flash if Pomrath mentions the name. I'm to be summoned immediately."

Leeward went off to take care of things. There was the end to Norm Pomrath's privacy, of course. From now until Quellen withdrew the Ear, Pomrath could not embrace his wife, relieve his bowels, scratch his armpit, or denounce the High Government without having some omniscient monitoring system making a record of it. Too bad, Quellen himself had been victimized by an Ear, and he knew the anguish of it, because that was how the treacherous Brogg had learned of the CrimeSec's illegal home in Africa. Yet Quellen had no real regrets about what he was doing to Pomrath. It was for Helaine's sake. She had asked to have Norm put in jail, hadn't she? This would be far less inconvenient to him. He'd never even know, most likely. And he might just lead Quellen to the source of the hopper enterprise. In any event it would be extremely difficult for Pomrath to take leave of the present century while he was being monitored.

Quellen dismissed the Pomrath problem from his mind, for the moment, and turned his attention to other matters of urgency.

The day's general crime reports had landed on his desk. Obsessed as he was with hoppers, Quellen still had responsibilities in other sectors. He was required to examine the details of all crimes committed within his zone of Appalachia, and to make recommendations for dispensation. The new stack was about the same size as yesterday's— crime was a statistical constant—and, Quellen knew, today's atrocities would be neither less nor more imaginative than yesterday's.

He leafed through the documents.

The roster of crimes no longer chilled Quellen, and that was the worst part of the job. A creeping loss of sensitivity was overtaking him year by year. When he had been young and new at this game, a fledgling Class Eleven just finding out what it was all about, the extent of man's capacity to do injury to man had numbed him. Now it was all statistics and coded tapes, divorced from reality.

The crimes tended to be motiveless. The benign High Government had removed most of the archaic causes for crime, such as hunger, want, and physical frustration. Everyone received a paycheck, whether he worked or not, and there was enough food for all, nutritious if not particularly tasty. No one was driven into banditry to support a starving family. Most addictive drugs were easily available. Sex of all varieties could be had cheaply at government-regulated cubicles. These measures were signs of maturity, so it was said. By making most things legal, the High Government had removed the need to commit illegalities.

True. The motives for crime were largely extinct. Crime itself, though, remained. Quellen had had ample proof of that melancholy sociological fact. Theft, murder, rape—these were amusements, now, not matters of need. The middle classes were shot through with criminality. Respectable Class Six burghers did the most hideous things. Plump matrons from Class Five households waylaid strangers in dark alleyways. Bright-eyed children took part in abominations. Even the officers of the law themselves, Quellen knew, circumvented authority by illegal acts, such as establishing second homes for themselves in reservations supposedly limited to Class Two personnel. Yet at least Quellen's own crime did no direct injury to other human beings. Whereas—

Here was the account of a Class Eight hydroponics man who was accused of a biological crime: unlawful insertion of living matter in the body of another human being. It was alleged that he had anesthetized a fellow technician, made a surgical opening in his body with an ultrasonic probe, and placed within a lethal quantity of a newly developed Asian carniphage that proceeded to devour the circulatory system of the victim, rampaging up one artery and down the next vein, flowing like flame through the web of vessels. Why? "To see his reactions," was the explanation. "It was quite instructive."

Here was a Class Six instructor in advanced hermeneutics at a large Appalachian university who had invited a nubile young student to his luxurious two-room apartment and upon her refusal to participate in sexual relations with him did inflict on her a short-circuit of the pain centers, after which he raped her and turned her loose, minus all sensory reactions. Why? "A matter of masculine pride," he told the arresting officer. "The Latin-American concept of *machismo*—"

He had his pride. But the girl would never feel sensation again. Neither pain nor pleasure, unless the damage could be undone by surgery.

And here, Quellen saw, was the seamy account of a gathering of believers in the cult of social regurgitation, which had ended in tragedy instead of mystical experience. One of the worshippers, impelled by fathomless motives of cruelty, had covertly intruded three crystals of pseudoliving glass in his cud before turning it over to his companions. The glass, expanding in a congenial environment, had penetrated the internal organs of the victims in a fatal fashion. "It was all a terrible error," the criminal declared. "My intention was to swallow one of the crystals myself, and so share with them the torment and the ultimate release. Unfortunately—"

The story touched a chord of shock in Quellen. Most of these daily nightmare tales left him unmoved; but it happened that his Judith was a member of this very cult, and Judith had been on his mind since Helaine's visit. Quellen hadn't seen Judith or even been in touch with her since his last return from Africa. And it might just as easily have been Judith who swallowed these devilish crystals of pseudoliving glass as the unknown victims listed here. It might even have been me, Quellen thought in distaste. I should call Judith soon. I've been ignoring her.

He looked on through the reports.

Not all of the current crimes had been so imaginative. There was the customary quota of bludgeonings, knifings, laserings, and other conventional assaults. But the scope for criminality was infinitely great, and fanciful atrocities were the hallmark of the era. Quellen turned page after page, jotting down his observations and recommendations. Then he pushed all the troublesome material aside.

He had not yet had a chance to look at the spool that Brogg had labeled Exhibit B in the hopper investigation. Brogg had said that it represented some tangential evidence of timetravel outside the recorded 1979–2106 zone. Quellen put the spool on and settled back to watch.

It consisted of Brogg's scholarly cullings of the annals of occultism. The UnderSec had compiled hundreds of accounts of mysterious appearances and apparitions, evidently under the assumption that they might represent time travelers of a prehopper phase. "I wish to suggest," Brogg's memorandum asserted, "that while the normal range of the time-transport apparatus lies within five hundred years of the present time, there have been instances when an overshoot resulted in transportation to a much earlier period."

Maybe so, Quellen mused. He examined the evidence in a mood of detached curiosity.

Exhibit: the testimony of Giraldus Cambrensis, chronicler, born at the castle of Manorbier in Pembrokeshire, circa A.D. 1146. Giraldus offered the tale of a red-haired young man who turned up unexpectedly in the house of a knight known as Eliodore de Stakepole in western Wales:

This strange man said his name was Simon. He took the keys from the seneschal, and took over, also, the seneschal's job; but he was so clever and finished a manager that nothing was ever lost or wanting in the house, which ever more became prosperous. If the master or mistress thought of something they would like, and did not even speak their thought, he read their minds and, hey presto, he got it, and no orders given him! He knew where they cached their gold and jewels. He would say to them: 'Why this niggard care of your gold and silver? Is not life short? Then enjoy it, spend your gold or you will die without enjoying life and the money you so cautiously hoard will do you no service.' He had an eye for the good opinion of menials and rustics, and he gave them the choicest food and drink ... This strange red-haired man set foot in no church, used no breviary, and uttered no Catholic word or religious sentiment. He did not sleep in the manor house; but was always on hand to serve and spring forward to give what was wanted.

The chronicler related that the Stakepole children were curious about this mysterious Simon, and took to spying on him around the grounds of the manor house:

And, one night, peering out from behind a holly bush, when the strange man was, by chance, gazing hard into the waters of a still mill dam, they saw him moving his lips as if in converse with something unseen.

Which was duly reported to the elder Stakepole, and that virtuous knight instantly summoned Simon to his private chamber and gave him the sack:

As they took the keys from him, the lady of the manor asked him: 'Who art thou?'
He replied: 'I am begotten of the wife of a yokel of this parish by a demon who lay upon her in the shape of her own husband.'
He named the man who was so cuckolded, who was lately dead. The mother was still alive, and when strict inquiry was made of her, the thing was certified to be true by her public confession.

Interesting, Quellen thought. Where did Brogg get these things? It could very well have been that the red-haired "demon" was a hopper accidentally hurled too far in time. So, too, these other monkish accounts. The twelfth and thirteenth centuries, according to Brogg's researches, had been a fertile era for the arrival of inexplicable strangers. Not all of them had arrived in human form, either. Quellen observed an extract from the *Eulogium Historiarum* prepared at Malmesbury Abbey, under the rubric A.D. 1171:

On the night of the birthday of the Lord, there were thunderings and lightnings of which the like had not been heard before. And at Andover, a certain priest, at midnight, in the presence of the whole congregation, was cast down by lightning, with no other injuries ... but what looked like a pig was seen to run to and fro between his feet. ...

Brogg had ferreted out a parallel case in the *Annales Francorum Regium* of the monk Bertin, inscribed circa A.D. 1160. The entry for A.D. 856 declared:

In August, Teotogaudus, Bishop of Trier, with clerics and people was celebrating the office when a very dreadful cloud, with thunderstorms and lightning, terrified the whole congregation in the church, and deadened the sound of the bells ringing in the tower. The whole building was filled with such dense darkness that one and another could hardly see or recognize his or her neighbor. On a sudden, there was seen a dog of immense size in a sudden opening of the floor or earth, and it ran to and fro around the altar.

Pigs? Dogs? Trial runs, perhaps, in the early days of the time-travel enterprise, Quellen wondered? The machine was still new and unreliable, he imagined, and hapless beasts had been placed within its field, and then had been spurted into the past to the consternation of the devout, devil-dreading citizens of the middle ages. A deplorable overshoot had taken the unhappy creatures back beyond the industrial revolution, but of course the operators of the machine could not have known the ultimate destinations of their passengers, unless they had had knowledge of these same records that Brogg had unearthed.

Nor did all Brogg's cases involve medieval episodes. A good many sections of Exhibit B dealt with instances more recent, through still well outside the 1979 date that had been considered the extreme limit of pastward travel. Quellen gave heed to the case of a girl who appeared at the door of a cottage near Bristol, England, on the evening of April 3, 1817, and begged for food in what was described as "an unknown language."

How did they know what she was begging for, then, Quellen asked himself? The spool did not answer. It informed him instead that the girl who spoke unintelligibly was brought before a magistrate, one Samuel Worral, who instead of arresting her on a vagrancy charge took her to his home. (Suspicious, Quellen thought!) He questioned her. She wrote replies in an unknown script whose characters looked like combs, birdcages, and frying pans. Linguists came to analyze her words. At length came one who described himself as "a gentleman from the East Indies." He interrogated her in the Malay language and received comprehensible replies.

She was, he declared, the Princess Caraboo, kidnapped by pirates from her Javan home and carried off to sea, involving her in many adventures before at length she made her escape on the English shore. Through the medium of the "gentleman from the East Indies," Princess Caraboo imparted many details of life in Java. Then a woman of Devonshire, a Mrs. Willcocks, came forward and announced that the Princess was actually her own daughter Mary, born in 1791. Mary Willcocks confessed her imposture and emigrated to America.

Brogg had appended the following speculation to the case of the Princess Caraboo:

"According to some authorities a multiple imposture was practiced here. A girl mysteriously appeared. A man stepped forward and claimed to understand her language. An older woman declared that it was all a fraud. But the records are faulty. What if the girl was a visitor from the future, and the 'gentleman from the East Indies' another hopper who shrewdly tried to pass her off as a Javan princess in order to keep her true origin from coming out, and the pretended mother yet another hopper who moved in to protect the girl when it looked likely that the Javan hoax would be exposed? *How many time-travelers were living in England in 1817, anyway?*"

It seemed to Quellen that Brogg was being too credulous. He passed on to the next instance.

Cagliostro: appeared in London, then in Paris, speaking with an accent of an unidentifiable kind. Supernal powers. Aggressive, gifted, unconventional. Accused of being in actuality one Joseph Balsamo, a Sicilian criminal. The same never proven. Earned a good living in eighteenth-century Europe peddling alchemistic powders, love philtres, elixirs of youth, and other useful compounds. Grew careless, was imprisoned in the Bastille in 1785, escaped, visited other countries, was arrested again, died in prison, 1795. Fraud? Impostor? Time-traveler? It was wholly possible. Anything, thought Quellen sadly, was possible once you began giving credence to such evidence.

Kaspar Hauser: staggered into the town of Nuremberg, Germany, on an afternoon in May, 1828. Apparently sixteen or seventeen years old. (A trifle young for becoming a hopper, Quellen thought. Perhaps deceptive in appearance.) Capable of speaking only two sentences in German. Given a pencil and paper, he wrote a name: "Kaspar Hauser." Assumption made that that was his name. He was unacquainted with the commonest objects and experiences of everyday affairs of human beings. Dropped down out of a time fault, no doubt.

A quick learner, though. Detained for a while in prison as a vagrant, then turned over to a schoolmaster, Professor Daumer. Mastered German and wrote an autobiographical essay, declaring that he had lived all his life in a small, dark cell, living on bread and water. Yet a policeman who had found him declared, "He had a very healthy color: he did not appear pale or delicate, like one who had been some time in confinement."

Many contradictions. Universal fascination in Europe; everyone speculating on the mysterious origin of Kaspar Hauser. Some said he was the crown prince of Baden, kidnapped in 1812 by the agents of the morganatic wife of his postulated father, the grand duke. Denied. Subsequently disproven. Others said he was sleepwalker, amnesiac. October 17, 1829: Kaspar Hauser found with a wound in forehead, allegedly inflicted by a man in a black mask. Policemen assigned to guard him. Several further purported assaults. December 14, 1833: Kaspar Hauser found dying in a park, with deep stab wound on his left breast. Claimed that a stranger had inflicted the wound. No sign of weapon in the park, no footprints in vicinity except Hauser's own. Suggestion that the wound was self-inflicted. Died several days afterward after exclaiming, "My God! that I should so die in shame and disgrace!"

Quellen disconnected the spool. Pigs, dogs, the Princess Caraboo, Kaspar Hauser—it was all quite entertaining. It might even support a belief that the whole of human history was besprinkled with time-travelers, and not simply the period from 1979 to 2106. Fine. But such facts did little to solve Quellen's immediate problems, however much the gathering of them had gratified the beefy Brogg's taste for scholarship. Quellen put the spool away.

He dialed Judith's number. Her face appeared on the screen, pale, somber, austere. She fell short of being beautiful by quite a good deal. The bridge of her nose was too high, her forehead was somewhat domed, her lips were thin, her chin was long. Her eyes were disquietingly far apart, with the right one slightly higher than the left. Yet she was not unattractive. Quellen had toyed with the temptation of allowing himself to fall in love with her. It was awkward, though; he could not let her get too far within his emotional defenses without telling her about the place in Africa, and he did not want to share that fact with her. She had a streak of righteousness; she might inform on him.

She said, "Have you been hiding from me, Joe?"

"I've been busy. Submerged in work. I'm sorry, Judith."

"Don't let your guilts overflow. I've been getting along quite well."

"I'm sure you have. How's your frood?"

"Dr. Galuber? He's fine. He'd like to have the chance to meet you, Joe."

Quellen bristled. "I've got no plans for entering therapy, Judith. I'm sorry."

"That's the second time you've said you were sorry in the last three sentences."

"I'm sor—" Quellen began, and then they both laughed.

Judith said, "I meant for you to meet Dr. Galuber socially. He'll be at our next communion."

"Which is?"

"Tonight, as a matter of fact. Will you come?"

"You know that social regurgitation has never delighted me very much, Judith."

She smiled in a wintry way. "I know that. But it's time you got out of your shell a little. You live too much to yourself, Joe. If you want to be a bachelor, that's your business, but you don't have to be a hermit too."

"I can put a piece in the slot of a frood machine and get advice just as profound as that."

"Maybe so. Will you come to the communion, though?"

Quellen thought of the case he had studied only an hour or so back, of the earnest communicant who had slipped pseudoliving glass into the alimentary canals of his fellow worshippers and then had watched them die in agony. He pictured himself writhing in torment while a weeping Judith clung to him and tried to extract the last vestige of empathic sorrow from his sufferings, after the manner of her cult.

He sighed. She was right: he had been living too much to himself these days. He needed to get out, away from his official responsibilities.

"Yes," he said. "Yes, Judith, I'll come to the communion. Are you happy?"

nine

Stanley Brogg had had a busy day.

The UnderSec was juggling a lot of Quellen's hot pota-toes at once, but it did not trouble him, for Brogg had a good capacity for work. He privately felt that he and Spanner between them kept the whole department going. They were two of a kind, both big men, massive and methodical, with a reserve of flesh to draw extra energy from in times of crisis. Of course, Spanner was in the administrative end, and Brogg a lowly legworker. Spanner was Class Six, Brogg Class Nine. Yet Brogg saw himself as Spanner's comrade-in-arms.

Those other two, Koll and Quellen—they were excres-ences on the department. Koll was full of hatred and mischief, seething with wrath simply because he was small and ugly. He had ability, of course, but his basically neurotic orientation made him dangerous and useless. If ever there was a case for compulsory frooding, it was Koll. Brogg often compared him to Tiberius Caesar: a baleful man full of menace, not insane but badly askew and so to be avoided.

If Koll were Tiberius, Quellen was Claudius: amiable, intelligent, weak to the core. Brogg despised his immediate superior. Quellen struck him as a ditherer, unfit for his post. Now and then Quellen could act with vigor and determination, but it didn't come naturally to him. Brogg had been doing the legwork for Quellen for years; other-wise, the department would long since have fallen apart.

A surprising thing about Quellen, though: he was capa-ble of criminality. That had startled Brogg. He didn't think the man had it in him. To obtain a plot of land in

Africa by diligently falsifying records, to apply and receive illegal stat service from a Class Seven apartment to the Congo, to live a secret life of ease and even luxury—why, it was an achievement so monstrously bold that Brogg still couldn't see how Quellen had carried it off. Unless the explanation was that Quellen was so repelled by the harshness of life all about him that he was willing to take any risk to escape from it. Even a coward could rise to what looked like moral grandeur in the interests of his own cowardice. In the same way, a soft, flabby man like the Emperor Nero could transform himself into a demon simply to preserve his own flabbiness. Nero, thought Brogg, hadn't been innately demonic after the fashion of Caligula; he had drifted into monstrosity in easy stages. In a way it was out of character for him, just as Quellen's surprising act of boldness jarred with the image of the man that Brogg had constructed.

Brogg had found out Quellen's great secret purely by accident, though there was some degree of treachery mixed into it. He had suspected for quite a while that Quellen was up to something peculiar, but he had no idea what it was. Deviant religious activity, perhaps; maybe Quellen belonged to one of the proscribed cults, a chaos group perhaps, or one of the rumored bands that gathered in dark corners to pray to the vicious pyrotic assassin, Flaming Bess.

Not knowing the details, but sensing the defensive wariness in Quellen's recent behavior, Brogg sought to turn the situation to his personal profit. He had high expenses. Brogg was a man with pretensions to scholarship; immersed as he was in the study of the ancient Romans, he had surrounded himself with books, authentic Roman coins, scraps of history. It took money to buy anything authentic. Brogg was living to the hilt of his salary now. It had struck him that Quellen might be a fruitful victim for extortion.

First Brogg, had spoken to Quellen's roommate of the time, Bruce Marok—for Quellen had not yet been promoted to Class Seven, and like any unmarried male of his class he was required to share an apartment. Marok, while confirming that something odd was going on, did not offer any details. He didn't seem to know much. Then came Quellen's promotion, and with the uptwitch Marok dropped out of the picture.

Brogg slapped an Ear on his boss and sat back to listen.

The truth came out soon enough. Quellen had connived to get a chunk of Africa registered under a blind name for which he was the nominee. Much of Africa had been set aside as a private reserve for members of the High Government—the tropical part, particularly, which had been generally depopulated during the Spore War a century and a half back. Quellen had his slice. He had arranged for a house to be built there, and for unauthorized stat service so that he could pop back and forth across the Atlantic in a twinkling. Of course, Quellen's little scheme was certain to be exposed eventually by one of the resurvey squads. But that part of the world was not due for a resurvey for some fifty years, by which time Quellen would be in little danger.

Brogg spent a fascinated few weeks tracking Quellen's movements. He had thought at first that Quellen must take women to the hideaway for participation in illicit cultist activities, but no, Quellen went alone. He simply sought peace and solitude. In a way, Brogg sympathized with Quellen's need. However, Brogg had needs of his own, and he was not a sentimental man. He went to Quellen.

"The next time you stat to Africa," he said blandly, "think of me. I envy you, CrimeSec."

Quellen gasped in shock. Then he recovered. "Africa? What are you talking about, Brogg? Why would I go to Africa?"

"To get away from it all. Yes?"

"I deny all your accusations."

"I've got proof," said Brogg. "Want to hear?"

In the end, they reached an accommodation. For a generous cash payment, Brogg would keep silent. That had been several months ago, and Quellen had paid regularly. So long as he did, Brogg observed the bargain. He was not really interested in informing on Quellen, who was much more useful to him as a source of money than he would be in an institution for corrective rehabilitation. Pursuing his studies more easily on Quellen's hush money, Brogg hoped earnestly that no one else would unmask the CrimeSec's secret. That would mean the loss of his extra income, and might even send him to jail too, as an accomplice after the fact. These days, Brogg watched over Quellen like a guardian angel, protecting him from the prying eyes of others.

Brogg knew that Quellen feared and hated him, of

course. It didn't trouble him. Secreted in various places throughout the vicinity were taped accounts of Quellen's iniquity, programmed to deliver themselves to High Government authorities in the event of Brogg's sudden death or disappearance. Quellen knew that. Quellen wasn't about to do anything. He was well aware that the moment the sensors of those devilish little boxes ceased to pick up the alpha rhythms of Stanley Brogg, autonomic legs would come forth and the telltales would march down to headquarters to pour forth their accusations. So Quellen and Brogg were at a standstill of mutual benefit.

Neither of them ever mentioned the situation. In the office, work proceeded serenely, though Brogg occasionally allowed himself a veiled reminder to keep Quellen uncomfortable. Generally Brogg took orders and carried them out.

As, for example, on this hopper business.

He had spent the last few days tracking Donald Mortensen, the potential hopper who was due to skip out on May 4. Quellen had asked Brogg to handle the Mortensen case with the greatest delicacy. Brogg knew why. He was clever enough to foresee the time-paradox consequences that might result if somebody interfered with the departure of Mortensen, who was on the documented hopper list. Brogg had gone over those old lists himself to compile the spool he had labeled Exhibit A. Subtract a man from the old records and the whole world might totter. Brogg knew that. Undoubtedly Quellen knew that too. Why, most likely Kloofman and Danton would have a dozen aneurysms pop in their aging arteries when they found out that Quellen's department was monkeying with the structure of the past. Such monkeying jeopardized everybody's status in the present, and those who had the most status to lose—the Class Ones—were the ones who would get most agitated over the investigation.

So Brogg was careful. He was pretty sure that the High Government would quash the Mortensen investigation once word of it got to Them. In the meanwhile, though, Brogg was merely carrying out his assignment. He could fry Quellen by botching the work and tipping off Mortensen; but Brogg had powerful motives for preserving Quellen from harm.

He found Mortensen easily: a lean, blonde man of twenty-eight, with pale blue eyes and eyebrows so white they were virtually invisible. Brushing against him at a quickboat ramp, Brogg managed to affix an Ear to the man, hanging the hooked patch of transponding equipment neatly in Mortensen's flesh. Brogg used a splinter model, working it into a callus in Mortensen's palm. The man would never feel it. In a few days it would dissolve, but meanwhile it would transmit a world of information. Brogg was expert at such things.

He tuned in on Mortensen and recorded his activities.

The man was involved with a person named Lanoy. Brogg picked up things like:

"—at the station with Lanoy on the hop day—"

"—Lanoy's fee is on deposit—"

"—you tell Lanoy that I'll be going out the first week in May—"

"—yes, at the lake, the place I met him the last time—"

Mortensen was married. Class Ten. Didn't like his wife. Hopping provided instant divorce, Brogg thought with amusement. The Ear gave him Sidna Mortensen's shrill complaints, and he couldn't help but agree that the best thing Mortensen could do was hop. Brogg compiled a considerable dossier on the potential hopper.

Then came The Word, from Kloofman via Giacomin via Koll to Quellen and thence to Brogg:

"Leave Mortensen alone. He's not to be tampered with. That's The Word."

Brogg looked questioningly at Quellen. "What should I do? We're learning a lot from Mortensen."

"Discontinue the investigation."

"We could chance carrying it on quietly," Brogg suggested. "So long as Mortensen takes no alarm, we'd continue to get data from him. I'm not suggesting that we actually interfere with his departure, but until—"

"No."

Coward, Brogg thought. Afraid the High Government will flay you!

In a moment of anarchy Brogg saw himself deliberately destroying Donald Mortensen, flying in the face of the High Government, possibly smashing everything like Samson putting his shoulders to the pillars of the temple. It would have amused Brogg to learn that the supposedly meek Quellen had had the same rebellious thought. There was tremendous power in knowing that the minor act of a minor official could threaten the security of the High Government. Yet Brogg did not give way to the impulse, any more than Quellen had. He obediently discontinued the Mortensen investigation. Mortensen would depart for the past on May 4, and the continuum would be preserved.

Anyway, Brogg had a new lead on Lanoy.

It had come to light today. A prolet named Brand, Class Fifteen, had had too much to drink in a common saloon. Leeward, refreshing himself in the drinker, had listened to Brand running off at the mouth about Lanoy and his hopper business. Without benefit of modern technology, Leeward thus picked up a vital clue and brought it to Brogg.

"Let's have Brand in for interrogation," Broog said when he heard what Leeward had done. "Get him here. No—wait. I'll get him. You cover the office."

Brogg went out for a reconnaissance. He scouted the drinker, saw Brand, calculated the imponderables. After some hesitation he cut Brand out from the herd, identified himself as a government man, and remanded the prisoner for interrogation. Brand looked frightened. "I didn't do nothing," he insisted. "I didn't do *nothing!*"

"There'll be no harm to you," Brogg promised. "We simply want to question you."

He took Brand into custody. When he reached the Secretariat building with the prolet, Brogg learned that Quellen had issued a new instruction.

"He wants an Ear put on his brother-in-law," Leeward said.

Brogg grinned. "Nepotism even in criminal investigations? Doesn't the man have any shame?"

"I couldn't answer that," said Leeward stolidly. "But he says that the brother-in-law is thinking of making a hop. He wants it checked. He wants an Ear on the fellow and round-the-clock monitoring, right away. Norman Pomrath's the name. I've already got the data on him."

"Good. We'll take care of Pomrath at once."

"Pomrath's supposed to be in contact with Lanoy, Quellen said."

"Looks like everybody's in contact with Lanoy. Even Quellen's been approached, did you know that?" Brogg laughed. "I haven't had a chance to tell him that Mortensen was dealing with Lanoy too, but I doubt that it'll surprise him. And this prolet here, this Brand you found— there's another lead to Lanoy. We're bound to trace one of them back to the source in another day or so."

"Do you want me to put the Ear on Pomrath?" Leeward asked.

"I'll do it," said Brogg. "I've got a gift for that kind of thing. You have to admit it."

Brogg certainly did. He could move gracefully for a man of his bulk. As sinuously as any dedicated *frotteur*, Brogg could approach a victim in a quickboat and gently introduce an Ear to the unlikeliest of places. It was a gift that had stood him in good stead when he set out to spy on Quellen; he had handled the Mortensen situation equally skillfully. Now Pomrath. Brogg went down to the laboratory and rummaged about for the most advanced model Ear that was available.

"Here's a beauty," the lab technician told him with pride. "We've just finished it. We've succeeded in melding Ear technology to a substrate of pseudoliving glass, and the result is unique. Take a look."

Brogg held out a fleshy palm. The technician dumped onto it a tiny metallic transponding plaque a few molecules in thickness, wholly invisible but snugly contained in a glossy little bead of some green plastic.

"What does it do?" Brogg asked.

"It functions normally as an Ear. But the spicule of the glass has a life-tropism of unusual character. Once the Ear is in place on the recipient's body, the glass goes into action and bores its way through the skin, generally looking for entry by way of the pores. It's a kind of artificial parasite, you see. It gets inside and stays there, where it can't possibly be removed by an itchy subject. And it broadcasts indefinitely. Surgical removal is necessary to shut off the information flow."

Brogg was impressed. There were plenty of models of Ear designed for internal use, of course, but they all had to be introduced through one of the bodily orifices of the victim, which presupposed certain difficulties for the agent. The usual method was to smuggle it into the victim's food. Since most people were reticent about eating in the presence of strangers, that required considerable planning. And in any event the Ear would be digested or excreted in short order. There were other bodily orifices, naturally, and Brogg had on occasion planted Ears in women who were off their guard in a throbbing moment of ecstatic passion, but the technique was a tricky one. This was infinitely better: to slap the Ear on externally, and let the device itself take care of the job of getting within the victim's body. Yes. Brogg liked the concept.

He spent an hour learning how to use the new model Ear. Then he went after Norm Pomrath.

The televector scanner located Pomrath quickly for him: at the Central Employment Register, doubtless punching the job machine in the customary prolet mood of total despair. Brogg changed into a shabby prolet tunic, suitable for Class Twelve slope vicinity, and headed for the domed building of the job machine.

He had no difficulty finding Pomrath in the crowd. Brogg knew approximately what the man was supposed to look like—stocky, dark, tense—and almost at once he found himself staring right at him. Brogg insinuated himself into the line not far from Pomrath and observed the CrimeSec's unhappy brother-in-law for a while. Pomrath spoke to no one. He peered at the red and green and blue banks of the job machine as though they were his personal enemies. His lips were tight with distress and his eyes were harshly shadowed. This man is in anguish, Brogg thought. No wonder he's planning to become a hopper. Well, we'll soon know a great deal about him, won't we?

Brogg sidled up behind Pomrath.

"Excuse me," he said, and stumbled. Pomrath reached out a hand to steady him. Brogg clasped his fingers around Pomrath's wrist and pressed the Ear firmly into the hairy skin just above the ulna. Straightening, he thanked Pomrath for his assistance, and all the while the pseudoliving glass in which the Ear was embedded was activating its tropism and drilling a path into Pomrath's living flesh.

By evening, the Ear would have migrated up Pomrath's arm to some nice warm fatty deposit where it could settle down and transmit its signals.

"Clumsy of me," Brogg muttered. He moved away. Pomrath did not show any sign of being aware that something had been affixed to him.

Returning to the office, Brogg examined the flow from the monitor device. Pomrath had left the job-machine building now, it appeared. The tracer line on the oscilloscope showed the minute neural explosions that told of footsteps. Pomrath walked for ten minutes. Then he halted. Complex muscular actions: he was entering a building with a manually operated door. Now came a voice pickup.

POMRATH: Here I am again, Jerry.

STRANGE VOICE: We got a couch all ready for you.

POMRATH: With a nice goddam hallucination, okay? Here I am fighting off the Crab People, you see, and there's this naked blonde panting to be rescued, while Kloofman is waiting to give me the Galactic Medal of Honor.

VOICE: I can't pick the effect for you, Norm. You know that. You pay your pieces and you get what comes. It's all what's stirring around inside your head that settles the picture for you.

POMRATH: There's plenty stirring around inside *my* head, pal. Where's the mask? I'm going to dream a beauty. Norm Pomrath, the destroyer of worlds. Disrupting time and space. The devourer of continua.

VOICE: You sure got a crazy imagination, Norm.

Brogg turned away. Pomrath was in a sniffer palace, evidently. Nothing meaningful was going to turn up on the monitor now—nothing but Pomrath asleep on the couch enjoying or perhaps not enjoying his hallucination.

In another room, Leeward was still interrogating the hapless prolet Brand. Brand looked disturbed. Brogg listened in for a while, found little of significance going on, and checked out for the day. Quellen had already gone home, he observed. To Africa, maybe, for the evening.

Brogg reached his own apartment in a short while. As required, he had a roommate—a legal assistant in one of the judiciary divisions—but they had managed to work things out so that their paths rarely crossed. You had to make the best accommodation you could to the existing living conditions.

Tired, Brogg got quickly under the molecular bath and cleansed himself of the day's grime. He programmed dinner. Then he selected a book. He was pursuing a fascinating theme in his favorite subject, Roman history: Tiberius' handling of the rebellion of Sejanus. The interplay of character was irresistible: Sejanus, the sly favorite of the sinister old Caesar, overreaching himself at last and being cast down from the heights of power by Tiberius, the Capri-dwelling old goat.

Easily, Brogg drifted into contemplation of those distant and violent events.

If I had been Sejanus, he thought, how would I have handled the situation? More tactfully, no doubt. I would never have provoked the old boy that way. Brogg smiled.

If he had been Sejanus, he knew, he would ultimately have come to hold the throne in his own name. On the other hand—

On the other hand, he was not Sejanus. He was Stanley Brogg of the Secretariat of Crime. More's the pity, Brogg thought. But we must make do with what we have.

ten

Night was closing in like a clamped fist. Quellen changed his clothes after a leisurely shower that used up nearly his entire week's quota of washing water. He dressed in clothes that were a bit on the gaudy side, in sullen rebellion against the sort of evening that Judith was going to inflict on him. The people who came to these communions of social regurgitation tended to be drab, consciously so. He despised their puritanical austerity. And so he donned a tunic shot through with iridescent threads, gleaming red and violet and azure as he shifted the angles of refraction.

He did not eat dinner. That would be an unpardonable faux pas, in view of this evening's planned ceremony. Still, he needed to keep his glucose level up after the tensions of the day. A few tablets took care of that. Refreshed, Quellen sealed his apartment and went out. He was meeting Judith at the communion. Afterward, perhaps, he might go home with her. She lived alone since she had joined him in Class Seven. It would be an act of good citizenship, Quellen knew, to marry her and combine their living quarters. Quellen was not prepared to be so patriotic just yet.

The cult session was being held, Judith had informed him, at the Class Four home of a certain Brose Cashdan, an administrator of the intercontinental stat nexus. It was interesting to Quellen that a transportation tycoon like Cashdan would get involved in such a cult. Of course, the cult of social regurgitation wasn't on the proscribed list. It might be esthetically distasteful, but it wasn't subversive like some of the others. Still, Quellen's experience with high administrators had taught him that they tended to be

97

guardians of the status quo. Maybe Cashdan was different. In any case, Quellen was curious about the house. He had not seen many Class Four homes.

Brose Cashdan's villa lay just within the inner zone of the Appalachia stat radius. That meant that Quellen could not reach it by the instantaneous transmission of the stat, but had to take a quickboat. A pity, that; it was a waste of half an hour. He programmed his course northward. The screen within the quickboat gave him a simulated view of what was below: the Hudson River, silvery and serpentine in the moonlight, and then the furry hills of the Adirondack Forest Preserve, a thousand acres of unspoiled wilderness in the middle of the sprawl of the city, and finally the floodlit glitter of the landing ramp. Local transport took Quellen speedily to Cashdan's place. He was a little late, he knew, but it did not bother him.

It was quite a villa. Quellen was not prepared for such opulence. Of course, Cashdan was required to live in just one location, unlike the Class Two people who could have several homes in scattered parts of the world. Still, it was a magnificent establishment, constructed mainly of glass with axial poles of some spongy, tough-looking synthetic. There were at least six rooms, a small garden(!), and a rooftop landing stage. Even from the air the place had a warm, inviting glow. Quellen stepped into the vestibule, peering ahead in hopes of catching sight of Judith.

A portly, sixtyish man with a starched white tunic came out to greet him. Diagonally across the tunic was emblazoned the golden sash of power.

"I'm Brose Cashdan," the man said. His voice was deep, the voice of authority. Quellen could see this man making brisk decisions all day long and scarcely bothering to get a recommend from a High Government official.

"Joseph Quellen. I was invited by—"

"Judith da Silva. Of course. Judith's inside. Welcome, Mr. Quellen. We're honored that you've chosen to join us. Come in. Come in."

Cashdan managed to sound ingratiating and commanding at the same time. He propelled Quellen into an inner room twenty feet long and at least thirty feet in width, carpeted wall-to-wall with some gray foamy substance that possibly had a degree of pseudolife. There was certainly nothing austere or drab about this shining palatial residence.

Eight or nine people sat clustered on the floor in the

very middle of the room. Judith was among them. To Quellen's surprise, Judith had not chosen to dress in the piously self-effacing manner that most communicants of this cult preferred. Obviously this upper-class gathering had different norms. She was wearing a highly immodest sprayon dress, blue with green undertones. A strip of fabric passed between her breasts, which otherwise were bare, and wound about her hips and loins. Her nakedness was covered, more or less, but since the covering was nothing but pigment she might just as well have come nude. Quellen understood that such extreme fashions were permissible only in sophisticated circles where the mode was Class Six or better. It was a trifle pushy, then, for Judith, a Class Seven, to expose herself this way. Quellen sensed that he and Judith might well be the only Sevens in the room. He smiled at Judith. She had small breasts, the desirable kind to have these days, and she had called attention to them by pigmenting her nipples.

Beside her sat a thick-bodied, practically neckless man with a clipped blue-stained beard, moist lips, and a placid expression. He was flanked by another woman, somewhat older than Judith, who wore a sprayon rig not much more modest than hers. On Judith it looked good; but not on this other one, who had unfashionably bulging breasts and plump haunches. She simpered at Quellen, who rudely started at her tastelessly exposed body.

The rest had a prosperous, earnestly intellectual look— mainly men, some of them a trifle on the epicene side, all of them well dressed and clearly high on the slope. Judith, rising to her feet, made the introductions. Quellen let most of the names glide past without sticking in his consciousness. The neckless man with the blue beard, he noted, was Dr. Richard Galuber, Judith's frood. The fleshy damsel was Mrs. Galuber. Interesting. Quellen hadn't known that the frood was married. He had long suspected that Judith was his mistress through some shameful reverse transference. Maybe so; but would Galuber bring his wife to meet his mistress at such a session? Quellen wasn't sure. Froods were often devious in their motivations, and for all Quellen knew Galuber was out to score some obscure therapeutic point on his wife by hauling her along.

Outside the group, Judith said, "I'm so glad you came, Joe. I was afraid you'd back out."

"I promised I'd come, didn't I?"

"Yes, I know. But you've got a tendency to withdraw from potentially hostile social experiences."

Quellen was annoyed. "There you go, frooding me again! Stop it, Judith. I came, didn't I?"

"Of course you did." Her smile was suddenly warm, authentically so. "I'm happy that you did. I didn't mean to impugn you. Come meet Dr. Galuber."

"Must I?"

She laughed. "As I said, you've got a tendency to withdraw from potentially—"

"All right. All right. Take me to Dr. Galuber."

They crossed the room. Quellen was unsettled by Judith's nakedness. A polymerized band of pigment wasn't clothing, really. He could make out the separate cheeks of her buttocks beneath the dark blue covering. It made her look more bare than actual nudity. The effect was provocative and disturbing. Her slender, angular body attracted him almost unbearably, especially in the social context of this urbane setting. On the other hand, Mrs. Galuber was just as exposed, practically, and Quellen's basic impulse was to throw a blanket over her shoulders to shield her shame.

The frood peered in a froodlike fashion at Quellen. "It's a delight to meet you, Mr. Quellen. I've heard a great deal about you."

"I'm sure you have," said Quellen nervously. He was disappointed that Galuber, despite his promisingly Teutonic name, did not fake the ritualistic Central European accent that most froods affected. "I didn't know that men in your profession belonged to cults like this."

"We accept spiritual experiences of all sorts," Galuber said. "Is there some reason why we should reject them?"

"Not really."

The frood nodded to his wife. "Jennifer and I have belonged to a social regurgitation group for more than a year, now. It's led us to some remarkable insights, hasn't it, beloved?"

Mrs. Galuber simpered again. She eyed Quellen in such a frankly sexual way that he rippled with shock. "It's been extremely enlightening," she agreed. Her voice was a warm, rich contralto. "Any kind of interpersonal communion is beneficial, don't you think? Which is to say, we achieve cathexis in the manner best suited to our needs." Jennifer Galuber's abundant flesh shook with genial laughter. Quellen found himself staring at the ugly upthrust mounds of her bare breasts, and he looked away, feeling guilty and sickened. The Galubers, he thought, must have a very odd marriage. But I will not let that fat witch sneak me off for a spot of instant interpersonal communion. Galuber may be bedding Judith, but it gains me nothing to bed his wife in turn, for the roles aren't equal.

Judith said, "I've been after Dr. Galuber to come to one of our communion group's meetings for months. But he's always resisted. He felt that until he and I had reached the right stage in my therapy, he couldn't let himself get involved on such an intimate level."

"There's more to it than that, of course," said the frood benevolently. "There always is. In this case, it was a matter of imposing my wife's handicap on the group, which would require special preparations. Jennifer's a galactose-deficient mutant, you see. She's got to stay on a galactose-free diet."

"I see," said Quellen blankly.

"It's a genetic fluke," Galuber went on. "She can't metabolize galactose at all, because of an enzyme deficit. Galactose precursors would pile up, and there'd be cell damage. So she's had to be on a galactose-free diet from birth, but that leads to other problems. Since there's the enzyme deficit, she can't synthesize galactose from endogenous carbohydrates, and if left uncompensated for that would lead to a partial replacement of galactolipids by glucolipids in the brain, a grossly defective blood group spectrum, poor immune reaction in organ transplants, abnormal brain development—oh, a great problem, in many ways."

"Can it be cured?" Quellen asked.

"Not in the sense of total remission of pathology. But it can be dealt with. Hereditary galactose metabolism defects can be controlled through enzyme synthesis. Nevertheless, she's got to remain on a special diet and avoid certain substances, among them the one that's the essence of tonight's ceremony. Which is why we had to substitute our own prepared material. An inconvenience to the host."

"Not at all, not at all," boomed Brose Cashdan unexpectedly. "A trivial matter! We're delighted that you could join with us, Mrs. Galuber!"

Quellen, bewildered by Galuber's stream of clinical verbiage, was relieved when Cashdan announced that the ceremony was about to begin. The frood had spouted all that stuff on purpose, Quellen thought resentfully, by way of establishing his intellectual supremacy. Instead of tossing forth the jargon of his own trade, which was easy enough to parry if you knew your way around cocktail-party froodianism, Galuber had chosen to engulf Quellen in a cascade of impenetrable technicalities of a medical sort. Quellen quietly cursed Jennifer Galuber's enzyme deficit, her wanton glances, her galactolipid accumulation, and her jiggling breasts. Slipping away from her, he followed Judith back across the room to the carpeted pit in the center where the ceremony was about to take place.

Judith said warningly, "Joe, please, don't back out the way you did the last time. You've got to learn to divorce yourself from tribal reactions. Look at things objectively. What's wrong with mixing a little saliva?"

"Nothing," he said. "I suppose."

"And digestive fluids—they can't harm you. It's all for the sake of spiritual communion. You mustn't look at things in obsolete ways."

"Is that how you get up the nerve to come naked to a social gathering?" he asked. "By looking at things in a non-obsolete way?"

"I'm not naked," she said primly.

"No. You're wearing a coat of paint."

"It conceals what society requires us to conceal."

"It leaves your secondary sex characteristics exposed," Quellen pointed out. "That's pretty naked."

"But not the primary ones. See for yourself. I'm perfectly covered in that area, and so, I'm well within the norms. Why don't you look at me? You can be so absurd at times, Joe."

Since she insisted on it, he stared at her waist. His eyes traveled as far as her thighs. He had to admit it: she was decently enough clad there. She looked nude, but she wasn't. Cunning, he thought. Provocative. He wondered how she got the sprayon outfit off. Maybe she would show him that, too, before the night was out. Her lean body held a powerful attraction for him. Unlike Helaine, whose leanness was the result of erosion and general haggardness, Judith's body was perfect in its lithe, slim elegance. Quellen would gladly have walked out right now with her.

But there was the ceremony to endure.

The members of this communion group assembled themselves on the rim of the carpeted pit. Brose Cashdan, as the host, produced a shining metallic bowl in which reposed a doughy mass about the size of a man's head. This, Quellen knew, was the substance of the love feast: an indigestible algae product with emetic properties. Adapted, no doubt, to suit Mrs. Galuber's galactose deficit.

Cashdan said, "Dr. Galuber has kindly consented to be our first celebrant this evening."

The lights were dimmed. Galuber took the gleaming bowl from Cashdan and rested it on his knees. Then, solemnly, he broke loose a fistful of the dough and crammed it into his mouth. He began to chew.

There were many cults. Quellen was no joiner, but even he had now and then been drawn into their ceremonies, generally through the urging of Judith. She drifted everywhere in her search for spiritual fulfillment—from frood to frood, from cult to cult. Quellen suspected that she had frequented the proscribed cults, perhaps even the outlawed Flaming Bess religion. He could picture Judith dancing naked—no flimflam of sprayon to cover her shame—while a grovelling pyrotic kindled an extrasensory blaze and raging voices called for the overthrow of the High Government. Pyrotics had actually assassinated several Class One leaders a generation ago. The cult still endured.

Mainly, though, the cults were more innocent things—revolting, perhaps, but not criminal. Such as this one, in which the chewing of the cud somehow led to a feeling of interpersonal harmony. Cashdan was intoning a digestive litany of some sort. Galuber was still stuffing resilient dough into his mouth. How much could that capacious belly hold? Jennifer Galuber was watching her husband with pride. The frood continued to devour. His face was transfigured, the eyes virtually sightless. Jennifer glowered. Her bare body seemed even more huge as she took vicarious pleasure from her husband's importance.

They were all chanting, now. Even Judith. Low, serious sounds of spirituality came from them.

She nudged him. "You too," she whispered.

"I don't know the words."

"Just drone along, then."

He shrugged. Galuber had ingested nearly every scrap of dough in the bowl. Surely his stomach was painfully distended, now. That stuff was like rubber. The emetic it contained worked on a critical-mass basis; once you had enough of the stuff in your gut, the peristalsis reflex was triggered and the sacred regurgitation began.

Judith, beside Quellen, was begging to be admitted into the realms of Oneness. Nirvana through upchucking, Quellen thought coldly. How could it be? What am I doing here? The chant rebounded from the glass walls and deafened him. In a subtle antiphony currents of sound were sweeping round and round the room. He could not avoid swaying in rhythm. His lips moved. He would have joined in, if only he knew the words. He found himself humming tunelessly, Cashdan, still leading the ceremony, stepped up his volume. His voice was a fine, thick, black basso, with plenty of intensity to it.

Galuber sat motionless in the center of the pit. His eyes were closed. His hands were clasped on his abdomen. His face was flushed. He alone was in stasis in the midst of this swaying, chanting congregation. Quellen forced himself to stay aloof, observing. He watched the rhythmic side-to-side motions of Jennifer Galuber's offensively large breasts. He watched Judith's fineboned face turn radiant with some inner ecstasy. A sexless young man with slicked-down maroon hair was jerking as though he had hold of a high-voltage wire. Around the room, the mysterious passion of social regurgitation was taking hold.

Dr. Galuber began to vomit, now.

The frood regurgitated with quiet dignity. His thick lips parted, and lumps of dough burst forth into the bowl. Sweat beaded his flushed face; there was effort in any kind of reverse peristalsis, even when the medulla was lulled, as it was by the drug within the dough. Yet he performed his function in the rite nobly. The bowl was filled.

It was passed around.

Hands clutched at moist dough. Take and eat, take and eat; here is the body, the authentic substance of the group. Join in the Oneness. Brose Cashdan was eating. Jennifer Galuber ate. Judith tranquilly accepted her portion. Quellen found a wet doughy mass in his hand.

Take. Eat.

Be objective. This is Oneness. His hand rose trembling toward his lips. He felt Judith's thigh warm against his own, beside him. Take and eat. Take and eat. Galuber lay prostrate in the pit, transfixed with ecstasy.

Quellen ate.

He chewed lustily, not allowing himself to hesitate. The

104

particular property of the indigestible substance was that it could be digested upon contact with saliva *following* immersion in the alimentary tract. One swallowing wasn't enough; Galuber had merely prepared it for their intake. Quellen swallowed. Oddly, he felt no queasiness. He had eaten ants, raw whelks, sea urchins, other exotic delicacies, and had not even been granted a chance of a spiritual experience in the bargain. Why hesitate at this?

The other communicants were weeping in joy. Tears glistened on Judith's sprayon garment. Quellen still felt deplorably objective about the universe. He had not joined the mystic communion after all, dutifully though he had observed the rite. He waited patiently for the ecstasy to pass from the others.

Judith whispered to him, "Will you celebrate the next round?"

"Absolutely not."

"Joe—"

"Please. I came, didn't I? I'm participating. Don't ask me to be the star."

"It's customary for strangers to the group to—"

"I know. Not me. Someone else can have the honor."

She looked reproachfully at him. Quellen realized that he had failed her. Tonight had been some sort of a test, and he had nearly passed. Nearly.

Brose Cashdan had produced a second mass of ritual dough. Without a word, Jennifer Galuber accepted the bowl and began to stuff herself. The frood, exhausted by his efforts, sat slumped wearily beside her, hardly watching. The rite proceeded as had the first. Quellen took part as before, without ever becoming involved in the action.

Afterward, Brose Cashdan approached Quellen and said softly, "Would you care to lead us in our next communion?"

"I'm sorry," said Quellen. "I really can't. I've got to leave soon."

"I regret that. We had hoped you'd participate to the fullest." Cashdan smiled dreamily and handed the bowl to someone else.

Quellen tugged at Judith's wrist and drew her to one side. "Come home with me," he whispered urgently.

"How can you think of sex *here?*"

"You aren't dressed chastely, you know. You've had two communions. Will you leave with me?"

"No," she said firmly.

"If I wait until the next communion is over?"

"No. Not then. You'll have to take communion yourself, as a celebrant, and *mean* it. Otherwise I'd feel no kinship to you later. Honestly, Joe, how can I give myself to a man I don't relate to? It would be so utterly mechanical—it would harm us both."

Her nakedness that was not nakedness stabbed at him. He could not bear to look down at the alluring slenderness of her body. With pain he said. "Don't do this to me, Judith. Play fair. Let's leave now."

For answer, she turned away and rejoined her companions in the ritual pit. The third communion was about to begin. Cashdan looked invitingly at Quellen, who shook his head and quickly left the room. Outside, he glanced back through the transparent wall and saw Judith with her head thrown back and her lips parted in rapture. The Galubers likewise looked ecstatic. The image of Jennifer Galuber's obese body burned its way indelibly into Quellen's brain. He fled.

He was home not long after midnight, but his apartment gave him no comfort. He had to escape. Recklessly, he stepped into the stat field and let himself be hurled to Africa.

Morning had come, there. A light mistlike rain was falling, but the golden gleam of the sun cut through the gray haze. The crocodiles were in their usual places. A bird screeched. The leafy boughs, heavy with rain, trailed toward the rich wet black earth. Quellen tried to let the peace of the place enfold him. Kicking off his shoes, he walked down to the edge of the stream. The muck oozed voluptuously between his toes. Some small insect nipped at his calf. A frog leaped into the stream, making a pool of widening concentric circles in the dark surface of the water. One crocodile lazily opened a glistening eye. The sweet, heavy air surged into Quellen's lungs.

He took no comfort in any of it.

This place was his, but he had not earned it. He had stolen it. He could have no real peace here. Behind him, in Appalachia, he likewise found no repose. The world was too much with him, and he was too little of the world. He thought of Judith, sensuous in sprayon, ecstatic as she chewed the cud. She hates me, Quellen thought, or perhaps she pities me, but the effect is the same. She'll never see me again.

He did not wish to remain in these pleasant surroundings while he was in such a mood.

Quellen returned to the stat. He stepped into the field, and was hurled back across the sea to his own apartment, leaving morning and entering the fist of night. He slept poorly.

eleven

At the office the following morning, Quellen found his two UnderSecs waiting for him with a third man, a tall, awkward, shabbily dressed fellow with a broken nose that projected beak-like from his face. Brogg had turned the oxy vent up to full, Quellen noticed.

"Who's this?" Quellen asked. "You've made an arrest?" Could it be, he wondered, that this was Lanoy? It didn't seem likely. How could this seedy prolet—too poor, apparently, to afford a plastic job on his nose—be the force behind the hoppers?

"Tell the CrimeSec who you are," Brogg said, nudging the prolet roughly with his elbow.

"Name is Brand," the prolet said in a thin, whiningly high voice. "Class Fifteen. I didn't mean no harm, it was just that he promised me a home all my own, and a job, and fresh air—"

Brogg cut him off. "We ran up against this man in a drinker. He had had one or two too many and was telling everyone that he'd have a job soon."

"That's what the fellow said," Brand mumbled. "Just had to give him two hundred credits and he'd send me somewhere where everyone had a job. And I'd be able to send money back to bring my family along."

"That can't be right," said Quellen. "Sending money back? Contact *up* the time-path?"

"That's what he said. It sounded so good, sir."

"A phony inducement," Brogg suggested. "If there's two-way contact, it upsets all our calculations. But there isn't any such thing."

Quellen said, "What was this fellow's name?"

108

"Lanoy, sir."

Lanoy! Lanoy everywhere, tentacles reaching in all directions at once!

Brand muttered, "Someone gave me this and told me to get in touch with him."

He held out a crumpled minislip. Quellen unfolded it and read it. It said:

OUT OF WORK?
SEE LANOY

"These things are everywhere," Quellen said. He reached into his own pocket and pulled out the slip he had been handed on the flyramp. Quellen had been carrying it around for several days like a talisman. He laid it beside the first. They were identical.

OUT OF WORK?
SEE LANOY

"Lanoy's sent a lot of my friends there," Brand said. "He told me they were all working and happy there, sir—"

"Where does he send them?" Quellen asked gently.

"I don't know, sir. Lanoy said he was going to tell me when I gave him the two hundred units. I drew out all my savings. I was on my way to him, and I just dropped in for a short one, when—when—"

"When we found him," Brogg finished. "Telling everyone in sight that he was heading to Lanoy to get a job."

"Mmm. Do you know what the hoppers are, Brand?"

"No, sir."

"Never mind, then. Suppose you take us to Lanoy."

"I can't do that. It wouldn't be fair. All my friends—"

"Suppose we *make* you take us to Lanoy," Quellen said.

"But he was going to give me a job! I can't do it. Please, sir."

Brogg looked sharply at Quellen. "Let me try," he said. "Lanoy was going to give you a job, you say? For two hundred units?"

"Yes, sir."

"What if we tell you that we'll give you a job for nothing? No charge at all, just lead us to Lanoy and we'll send you where he was going to send you, only free. And we'll send your family along too."

Quellen smiled. When it came to handling the lower prolets, Brogg was a far better psychologist than he was. He was forced to admit that.

"Sounds fair," Brand said. "Only I feel bad about it. Lanoy was nice to me. But if you say you'll send me for nix—"

"Quite right, Brand."

"I'll do it, then. I guess."

Quellen turned down the oxy vent. Brogg gestured to Leeward, who led Brand out of the room. Quellen said, "Let's go before he changes his mind. He's obviously wavering."

"Are you coming with us, sir?" Brogg asked. There was just a hint of sarcasm behind Brogg's obsequious tones. "It'll probably be a pretty filthy part of town. Vermin all over the place. The criminal section—"

Quellen scowled. "You're right," he said. "No need for me to go. You two take him. I've got plenty to do here."

As soon as they were gone, Quellen rang Koll.

"We're hot on the trail," he said. "Brogg and Leeward have traced a lead to the man who's behind the hoppers. They've gone out to make the arrest."

"Fine work," Koll said coldly. "It should be an interesting investigation."

"I'll report back to you as soon as—"

"Let it go for a while. Spanner and I are discussing departmental status changes. We'd prefer not to be disturbed during the next hour." He hung up.

What did that mean, Quellen wondered? The coldness in Koll's voice—well, that was nothing unusual, but it was significant. Koll had been harrying him all week for progress on the hopper business. Now that some progress had finally been made—now that a man was in custody who could lead them to the elusive Lanoy—Koll had been brusque, almost totally uninterested. Koll's hiding something, Quellen thought.

His conscience pricked him. The instant suspicion returned: Koll knows about Africa. That trip I made last night was monitored, and it was the last chunk of evidence in the case against me. Now they're getting the indictment ready.

No doubt Brogg had been offered a bigger price to talk than Quellen had been giving him to be silent, and he had sold out to the highest bidder. Koll knew everything, now. Demotion would be the least of Quellen's punishments.

110

Quellen's offense was a unique one. No one else, to his knowledge, had been shrewd enough to find that particular way out of heavily overpopulated Appalachia, the octopus of a city that spread all over the eastern half of North America. Of all the hundreds of millions of inhabitants of Appalachia, only Joseph Quellen, CrimeSec, had had the cleverness to find a bit of unknown and unregistered land in the heart of Africa and build himself a second home there. That was something for pride. He had the standard Class Seven cubicle of a room in Appalachia, plus a Class Two villa beyond the dreams of most mortals, beside a murky stream in the Congo. It was nice, very nice, for a man whose soul rebelled at the hellish conditions of Appalachian life.

But it took money to keep people bribed. Quellen had silenced everyone concerned who might know that he was living luxuriously in Africa instead of dwelling in a ten-by-ten cubicle in Northwest Appalachia, like a good Seven. Someone—Brogg, he was sure—had sold him out to Koll. And now Quellen was on very thin ice indeed.

A demotion would rob him even of the privilege of maintaining a private cubicle, and he would go back to sharing his home, as he had with the unlamented roommate Bruce Marok. It hadn't been so bad when Quellen had been below Class Twelve and had lived, first in the public bachelor dorms, then in gradually more private accommodations. He hadn't minded the presence of other people so much when he was younger. But when he had reached Class Eight and was put into a room with just one other person, that had been the most painful time of all, souring Quellen permanently.

In his own way, Marok was undoubtedly a genuinely fine fellow, Quellen reflected. But he had jarred on Quellen's nerves, crucifying him with his sloppiness and his unending visiphone calls and his constant presence. Quellen had longed for the day when he would reach Seven and could live alone, no longer with a roommate as a constant check. Then he would be free—free to hide from the inpressing crowd.

Did Koll know the truth? Quellen soon would find that out.

Restlessly he walked down the echoing corridor to the monitoring wing. Might as well find out what they've learned about Norm, he thought. The brown metal gate slithered into its slot as Quellen palmed the door identification plaque. He went in. Instruments hummed all over the place. Technicians salaamed to him. The smell of some antiseptic chemical was in the air, as though this were a hospital.

"The Pomrath monitor bank," Quellen said.

"This way, CrimeSec."

"Who's watching it?"

"It's been on automatic, sir. Here we are." The man pulled out a pneumochair. Quellen planted himself before the turning spools of a tape pickup. The technician said, "Would you like to plug in on realtime first, or go over what we've taped since last night?"

"I'll do a little of both," Quellen said.

"This is the realtime jack, and this—"

"I know. I've used the equipment before."

The technician colored and went scuttering away. Quellen jacked himself into the realtime circuit, and abruptly jacked himself out again. His brother-in-law was performing natural bodily functions. Quellen bit his lip. With a quick, edgy manipulation he activated the reserve spools and tuned in on what Norm Pomrath had been up to since Brogg had planted the Ear on him.

Quellen could not allow himself a one-to-one realtime correlation, of course, with Pomrath's activities. He had to be selective. Skimming along the tape, he found remarkably little conversation recorded. Pomrath had been to a sniffer palace last night. Then he had gone home. He had quarrelled with Helaine. Quellen listened.

POMRATH: I don't give a damn. I need my relaxation.

HELAINE: But we've waited dinner for you. And here you are all full of drugs. You don't even have an appetite!

POMRATH: What of it? I'm here. Put out the dinner. You program, I'll eat!

There was more of it, all relentlessly domestic and dreadfully dull. Quellen skipped ahead fifteen minutes and found the quarrel still going on, punctuated now by the snuffling sound of his nephew's tears and the annoyed comments of little Marina. It pained Quellen that the family disputes of the Pomraths should be so commonplace. He moved the tape on a short distance. The Ear had picked up different sounds. Harsh breathing sounds.

HELAINE: Put your hand there again.

POMRATH: Oh, honey, you know I will.

HELAINE: Right there. Oh! Oh, Norm!

POMRATH: Are you ready yet?

HELAINE: A little while. Give me time. This is so nice, Norm.

Quellen stared shamefully at the floor. A faintly incestuous pleasure went through him as he eavesdropped on the lovemaking of the Pomraths. He reached for the dial, hesitated, listened to sudden pangs of ecstasy, clenched his jaws together as the words on the tape became more intimate and then dissolved into a rush of gasping sighs.

I ought to erase this section, Quellen thought. I ought at least not to listen to it myself. How disgustingly curious we can get sometimes!

With a quick jerky motion he sped the dial ahead. Nothing but sleep-sounds now. Then morning-sounds. Children pattering around. Pomrath under the molecular bath. Helaine yawning, asking about the breakfast menu.

POMRATH: I'm going out early today.

HELAINE: You think you have a line on that job opportunity?

POMRATH: What job opportunity?

HELAINE: You know, the minislip you were carrying. About the man to see if you're out of work.

POMRATH: Oh. Him.

Quellen waited for more. The telemetry showed unusual excitement in Pomrath, a surge of pulse intensity, a rise in skin temperature. Nevertheless, the conversation was truncated without any word about Lanoy. Quellen skimmed again. The timer told him that he was approaching realtime levels now. Quellen jacked in once more.

POMRATH: You can take me to Lanoy, can't you?

The monitor was programmed to trip an alarm when the name "Lanoy" was mentioned. There was an imperceptible lag while the computer analyzed the wave forms of Pomrath's speech, and then the alarm went off. A red light began to glow on the control panel of the monitor system. Signals blared around the room. A warning bell sounded. *Pong Pong.*

Three technicians came running toward the instrument. *Pong.*

Quellen said, "It's all right. I'll monitor it. Just shut off these damned alarms."

Pong. Pong.

Quellen leaned forward, and sweat poured down the palms of his hands as he listened to his brother-in-law commit the ultimate betrayal of his family.

113

Pomrath had traveled a considerable distance that morning, unaware, of course, that his motions were being transmitted to the headquarters of the Secretariat of Crime and that his words and even his heartbeats were being recorded.

In the past several days he had asked many questions, mostly prior to the mounting of the Ear in his flesh. The minislips advertising Lanoy's services were widely distributed. Information about the actual whereabouts of Lanoy was not so easily had. But Pomrath had persistence.

He was determined to leave, now.

He had had all he could take. It was too bad about Helaine, of course, and the kids. He'd miss them. Yet he was fed up, and he sensed that he was on the edge of psychotic collapse. Words were losing their meaning for him. He'd stare up at a faxtape for half an hour, trying to puzzle out the significance of the rows of symbols on the yellow sheet. They had become squirming microbes to him. KLOOFMAN. UNEMPLOYMENT. TAX RATE. DANTON. MANKLOOF. LOYPMEMUNTNE. TONDAN. XAT RAET. KL. OOF. PLOYM. AX R. Dancing animalcules. EMPL. FMAN. Time to get away, ANTO. UNEM, TNEM. FLOOK. FLOOK! FLOOK! FLOOK!
KLOOF!

A simpler world, that's what he needed. To hop to a place not yet this fouled with humanity—yes. Yes. Lanoy was the answer. Pomrath's head throbbed. It seemed to him that his frontal lobes were swelling, pushing against his forehead dangerously forward. "Can you direct me to Lanoy?" His head might burst, spewing brains all over the street. "I'm out of work. I want to see Lanoy." FLOOK! XAT RAET! "Lanoy?"

A squat, flabby-faced man with a row of natural teeth on top and a single seamless chopper below said, "I'll get you to Lanoy. Four pieces, huh?"

Pomrath paid him. "Where do I go? What do I do?"

"Quickboat. Number Sixteen Line."

"Where do I get off?"

"Just get on, that's all."

EMPL! FMAN! Pomrath headed for the quickboat ramp. He filed obediently aboard. It seemed a pleasant coincidence that someone would have been so conveniently available to tell him how to reach the elusive Lanoy, Norm thought. But a moment's reflection led him to think

114

it was no coincidence at all. The flabby-faced man had probably been an agent of Lanoy, haunting him, ready to guide him in the right direction when the critical moment approached. Of course. His eyes were aching. Something coarse and gritty was in the air, a special eyeball-abrasive gas, perhaps, released by order of the High Government to bring about universal polishing of proletarian corneas. MANK! NOTD! Pomrath huddled in a corner of the quickboat. A cowled figure came up to him, a girl with shaven scalp, jutting cheekbones, no lips at all. "For Lanoy?" she asked.

"Why not?"

"Transfer to the Northpass Line."

"If you say so."

"It's the only way." She smiled at him. Her skin seemed to change color, cycling attractively through the spectrum from infragreen to ultralemon. PLOYM! XAT! Pomrath trembled. He wondered what Helaine would say when she knew. Would she weep? How soon would she remarry? Would his children bear his name? The line of Pomraths extinct? Yes. Yes. For he would have to bear some other name back there. FMANK! What if he called himself Kloofman? Sublime irony: my great-grandchild a member of the High Government. Some chance.

Pomrath got off the quickboat. The cowled girl remained aboard. How did they know who he was and where he was bound? He felt frightened. The world was full of specters. Pray for the repose of my soul, he thought. I'm so tired. OOF! TON!

He waited at the ramp. Around him the spires of ugly buildings of the previous century stabbed holes in the sky. He was out of the central slum-clearance zone now. Who knew what stinking warren he was heading toward? A new quickboat arrived. Pomrath boarded it unquestioningly. I am in your hands, he thought. LANOY! YONAL! Anyone. Anyone. Just get me out of here.

Out!

He journeyed northward. Was this still Appalachia? The sky was dark here. Programmed for rain, perhaps. A clean flush to purify the streets. What if Danton recommended a rain of sulfuric acid? The pavement hissing and smoking, citizens running to and fro as their flesh dissolved. The ultimate population control. Death from the skies. Serve you right for going outdoors. The quickboat halted. Pomrath got out and waited on the ramp. Rain was falling here, pocking against the sidewalk.

"I'm Pomrath," he said to a kindly old lady.

"Lanoy's waiting. Come on."

He found himself in rural surroundings ten minutes later. There was a shack by the edge of a lake. Figures moved mysteriously in and out. Pomrath was thrust forward. A purring voice said, "Lanoy's waiting for you out back."

He was a small man with a big nose. He wore clothing that seemed to be two hundred years old.

"Pomrath?"

"I think so."

"What are you, Class Twelve?"

"Fourteen," Pomrath confessed. "Get me out of here, will you please?"

"My pleasure," said Lanoy.

Pomrath looked at the lake. It was a hideous sight, crawling with pollution. Great greasy swatches of coarse algae roiled in the oily water.

Lanoy said, "Isn't it lovely? Six centuries of nonstop pollution interspersed with high-sounding official speeches. The renewal zone is still twenty years away by public count. Would you like to take a swim? We don't practice baptism here, but we can arrange a ceremony to fit anybody's religious preferences."

Pomrath shuddered. "I can't swim. Just get me out of here."

"The alga is *cladaphora*. Biologists sometimes come up here to admire it. It reaches lengths of ninety feet. We've also got anaerobic sludgeworms here, and fingernail clams. Quite primeval. I don't know how they survive. You'd be shocked if you knew the oxygen content of that water."

"Nothing shocks me," said Pomrath. "Please. Please."

"It's full of coliform intestinal bacteria also," Lanoy remarked. "I believe the current count is 10,000,000 per 100 milliliters. That's about 10,000 times the safe level for human contact. Lovely? Come inside, Pomrath. You know it's not easy, being a hopper."

"It's not easy being anything, these days."

"Consider the challenges, though." Lanoy led him within the shack. Pomrath was startled to see that the interior was out of keeping with the weatherbeaten exterior. Inside, everything was neat, spanking clean. A partition

116

divided the building into two huge compartments. Lanoy dropped into a web and lay there, jiggling, like a spider. Pomrath remained standing. Lanoy said, "I can take you and dump you into the year 1990, if you'd like, or 2076, or most any other year. Don't be fooled by what you read in the faxtapes. We're actually more versatile than the public knows. We're improving the process constantly."

"Send me anywhere," said Pomrath.

"The correct term is *anywhen*. But look here: I send you to 1990. Can you face it? You won't even be able to speak the language properly. You'll speak a weird jargon that they won't understand, all your grammar blurred. Do you know the distinction between 'who' and 'whom'? Between 'shall' and 'will'? Can you handle tenses?"

Pomrath could feel the blood surging in his arteries. He did not understand why Lanoy was weaving this cocoon of words about him. He had had enough words.

Lanoy laughed. "Don't let me frighten you. You don't need to know those things. They were forgotten, even then. People were sloppy in their speech. Not as sloppy as we are today, because we've had another few hundred years to erode the language. But they had blotted out all the conjugations and declensions already. Still, it'll take you a couple of weeks to learn how to communicate. You can get into a lot of trouble in a couple of weeks. Are you prepared to be sent to a lunatic asylum? Shock treatments, straight-jacket, all the barbarities of our ancestors?"

"Just get me out of here."

"The police will interrogate you. Don't give them your right name, Pomrath. You aren't listed in the hopper records, which means you never gave them your right name, and don't you dare try to do it. Make up a name. You can admit to being a hopper if you land in 1979 or later. If you go back earlier, you're entirely on your own. Frankly, I wouldn't try it. I don't think you've got the caliber for a free-lance trip like that. You're an intelligent man, Pomrath, but you're worn thin by care. Don't take risks. Go as an orthodox hopper and throw yourself on the mercies of the past. You'll make out."

"What does it cost?"

"Two hundred units. A token fee, really. Barely covers the energy costs."

"Is it safe?"

"As safe as taking a quickboat ride." Lanoy grinned.

117

"It's disconcerting. No High Government to watch over you. Dozens of independent national states. Local rivalries. Conflicting taxing bodies. You'll have to cope, but that's all right. I think you'll manage."

"It can't be worse than what's here."

"Are you married, Pomrath?"

"Yes. Two children. I love them deeply."

"Want to take the whole family along?"

"Can it be done?"

"With uncertainties. We've got to send you separately: mass limits. You could get scattered over a range of as much as a dozen years. Your kids arriving first, then you and your wife a few years later, maybe."

Pomrath trembled. "Suppose I go first. Will you keep a record of where I'm sent—*when* I'm sent—so that my family can come after me if that's what my wife wants to do?"

"Of course. We look out for your welfare. I'll get in touch with Mrs. Pomrath. She'll have the option of following you. Not many wives do it, of course, but she'll have the option. Well, Pomrath? Still with us?"

"You know I am," Pomrath said.

Quellen, monitoring the conversation, sat trancelike and chilled. He could not see Lanoy, he had no real idea where the conversation was taking place, but yet he realized that his brother-in-law was about to enroll in the legion of hoppers, and there was nothing that could be done about it. Unless Brogg and Leeward reached Lanoy's headquarters in the nick of time, and came bursting in to make the arrest—

A voice said, "Sir, UnderSec Brogg is calling."

Quellen pulled himself away from the monitor. A visionless phone was rolled up. Quellen put it to his ear.

"Where are you?" he demanded. "Have you traced Lanoy yet?"

"We're working on it," Brogg said. "It turned out Brand didn't know the exact location. He just knew somebody who could take him to somebody who could bring him to Lanoy."

"I see."

"But we've got a geographical area pegged. We're cordoning it and closing in by televector. It's only a matter of time now before we put the intercept on Lanoy in person."

"How much time?" asked Quellen icily.

"I'd say six hours," Brogg replied. "Plus or minus ninety minutes. We're certain to nail him today."

Six hours, Quellen thought. Plus or minus. And then Lanoy would be in custody.

But Norm Pomrath would be a hopper by then.

twelve

Brogg said in a relaxed tone, "I have to arrest you, of course. You understand that. It's regulations."

"Of course," Lanoy said. "It goes almost without saying. I wondered what took you people so long to get to me."

"Uncertainty in high places. There was a lot of dithering." Brogg smiled at the little man. "I don't mind telling you, you have the High Government quite upset. They're sweating to arrest you, but at the same time they're afraid of wrecking their position of power through some sort of rearrangement of past events. So they've been stalemated. It's the classic conflict situation: they must stop you, and they don't dare it."

"I appreciate their troubles," said Lanoy. "It's a terribly complicated life even for Them, isn't it? Well, you're here, now. Come outside. Let's watch the sunset, shall we?"

Brogg followed Lanoy from the shack. It was late, now, well into his overtime phase, but Brogg did not object. All day long he and Leeward had zeroed in on Lanoy, juggling televector constants until they had located him within a narrowing radius. As Brogg had told Quellen earlier in the day, it was only a matter of hours. In fact, it had taken four hours and some minutes from the time of Brogg's call. Deftly, Brogg had sent Leeward off on a wild goose chase an hour ago. Now Brogg and Lanoy were alone at this remote shack. Brogg had much to say to the hopper man.

A swollen golden sun hung suspended in the darkening sky. The track of illumination cast a purplish glow over the polluted lake. It took on an eerie glitter, and the

120

slime-creatures that writhed on its surface seemed ennobled by the aura of the dying day. Lanoy stared raptly into the west.

"It *is* beautiful," he said finally. "I could never leave this era, UnderSec Brogg. I see the beauty within the ugliness. Regard that lake. Was there ever anything like it? I stand here at sunset each night in awe."

"Remarkable."

"Very. There's poetry in that ooze. The oxygen's just about gone, you see. There's been a devolution of organic life there, so that we've got only anaerobic forms. I like to think that the sludgeworms dance down there at sunset. About, about, in reel and rout. Look at the play of colors on that big swatch of algae. It grows as long as seaweed here. Do you care for poetry much, Brogg?"

"My passion's for history."

"What period?"

"Roman. The early Empire. Tiberius through Trajan, approximately. Trajan's time: a true golden age."

"The Republic doesn't interest you?" asked Lanoy. "The brave puritans? Cato? Lucius Junius Brutus? The Gracchi?"

Brogg was astounded. "You know such things?"

"I cast a wide net," said Lanoy. "You realize that I deal with the past on a daily basis. I've acquired a certain familiarity with history myself. Trajan, eh? You'd like to visit Rome of Trajan's era, would you?"

"Of course," Brogg said huskily.

"What about Hadrian? Still a golden age there. If you couldn't have Trajan, would you settle for Hadrian? Let us say, a margin of error covering a generation—we might miss Trajan, but in that case we'd land somewhere in Hadrian. We'd do better to aim for the forward end of Trajan's rule. Otherwise the error might take us the other way, and you wouldn't like that, eh? You'd come out in Titus, Domitian, one of that nasty bunch. Not at all to your liking."

Brogg could manage only a hoarse, croaking voice. "What are you talking about?"

"You know quite well." The sun had set. The magic glow ebbed from the ruined lake. "Shall we go in?" Lanoy asked. "I'll show you some of the equipment."

Brogg allowed himself to be led back inside. He towered over the little man; Lanoy was no bigger than Koll, and had something of Koll's nervous inner energy. Yet

Koll brimmed with hatred and pustulence; Lanoy seemed utterly confident, with a core of tranquility within his active dynamism.

Lanoy opened a door in the partition that divided the building. Brogg peered in. He saw vertical bars of some gleaming material, an openwork cage, dials, switches, an array of rheostats. Rows of color-coded panels on the machinery radiated bright glows of data. It all seemed to be put together with an eye toward deliberate confusion.

"This is the time-travel machine?" Brogg asked.

"Part of it. There are extensions both in time and space. I won't plague you with the details. The principle is simple, anyway. A sudden strain on the fabric of the continuum; we thrust present-day material in, scoop out an equal bucketload of mass from the past. Conservation of matter, you understand. When our calculations are off by a few grams, it causes disturbances, implosions, meteorological effects. We try not to miss, but we sometimes do. There's a fusion plasma at the heart of it all. No better way to rip open the continuum; we use our own little sun to do it. We tap off the theta force, you see. Every time someone uses a stat, it builds up temporal potential that we grab and utilize. Even so, it's an expensive process."

"What do you charge for a trip?"

"Two hundred units, generally. That is, if we're willing to take money at all."

"You send some people free?" Brogg asked.

"Not exactly. We won't accept the money of certain individuals, I mean. We insist on payment of a different kind—services, information, that sort of thing. If they're not willing to render what we need, we don't transport them. For those people, no amount of money could hire us."

"I don't altogether follow."

"You will," Lanoy said. He closed the partition and returned to the office part of the shack. Sprawling out comfortably in his web, he asked Brogg, "What arrest procedure are you going to follow in my case?"

"You'll have to come down to the office to talk to CrimeSec Quellen. He'll have disposition of the case. Meanwhile we'll have to cordon this place off with a wide-band radion, and it'll remain sealed pending appeal. Any habeas corpus will go automatically to the High Government. Of course, if you can handle Quellen, the picture will change completely."

122

"But I must go to the office?"

"Yes."

"What sort of man is this Quellen. Malleable?"

"I think so. Especially if you use the right hammer on him," Brogg said.

"Does the hammer have a high rental cost?"

"Not very high." Brogg leaned forward. "Is your machine really limited to a reach of only five centuries?"

"Not at all. We keep improving. We've had a controlled reach of five centuries for quite some time, but an uncontrolled reach that's much greater."

"Yes," said Brogg. "The pigs and dogs thrown back to the twelfth century, and such."

"You know about those?"

"I've been very thorough. What's your controlled reach now?"

Lanoy shrugged. "It's variable. We can hit almost anywhere in two thousand years, but the built-in error gets wider the further the throw. We've got it down to plus or minus thirty years now, but that's quite a range. At the furthest, that is. We could hit 1492 or 1776 smack on the nose, I firmly believe." He smiled. "What's the hammer for pounding Quellen?"

"It'll cost you," said Brogg. "What's the cost of a ticket to Hadrian?"

"The hammer for Quellen."

"You won't take cash?"

"Not from you."

Brogg nodded. "Let's negotiate," he said. "I think we can strike a deal."

By sunset, Helaine Pomrath was convinced that her husband had become a hopper.

It was almost a telepathic thing. He had not come home for dinner, but he had been late for dinner quite frequently the last few weeks. Yet this was different. Helaine felt a strange sense of his absence. She had shared her life with him for so long that she had grown accustomed to his presence, even when he was not with her physically. Now she felt herself in the company of the presence of his absence.

The room seemed smaller, darker. The children's eyes were wide. Helaine said reassuring things to them. She tried not to think of Beth Wisnack and her grim prophecy that Norm was soon to become a hopper. Helaine asked the time, and the earwatch told her that it was half past eighteen. She gave the children their dinner, but did not eat herself.

At quarter after nineteen, she phoned her brother at his apartment.

"I hate to disturb you, Joe, but it's about Norm. He isn't home for dinner, and I'm worried."

There was a long silence at the other end. Helaine watched Quellen's face, but the expression on it baffled her. His lips were tightly compresed.

"Joe? Why aren't you answering me? Listen, I know I'm just a foolish woman who's worrying about nothing at all, but I can't help it. I've got this definite feeling that something terrible has happened."

"I'm sorry, Helaine. I did what I could."

"What are you talking about?"

"There's been an arrest. We've pulled in the slyster who ran the hopper outfit. But there just wasn't time to get Norm. He slipped right through."

She felt the chill sweeping up from her legs and invading her internal organs, turning them one by one to lumps of resonating ice. "Joe, I don't understand you. Do you know something about Norm?"

"We were monitoring him. Brogg put an Ear on him last night at my instruction. He went out to look for Lanoy this morning. The slyster."

"The one you arrested?"

"Yes. Lanoy's running the hopper game. *Was* running. He's in custody. I'll be interrogating him in the morning. Norm went to him. It was far out—the trip took him all morning. We were vectoring in on Lanoy, you understand, but there was absolutely no way to get to Norm in time. I've got a tape of the whole thing as it came out of the Ear."

"He's—gone?"

"Gone," Quellen said. "His destination was 2050. Lanoy wasn't sure that they could hit the year exactly, but he said the odds were in favor. I want you to know, Helaine, that Norm was thinking of you right up until he left. You can listen to the tapes yourself. He said he loved you and the children. He was trying to arrange things so you and the children could follow him to 2050. Lanoy agreed to do it. It's all on record."

"Gone. He just hopped like that."

"He was in bad shape, Helaine. The things he was saying this morning—he was practically insane."

"I know it. He's been like that for days. I tried to get him to go to a frood, but—"

"Is there anything I can do, Helaine? Do you want me to come over and stay with you?"

"No."

"I can have a registered consolation service come around."

"Don't bother."

"Helaine, you've got to believe me, I did everything that was in my power to prevent this from happening. And if you choose to follow him the hopper way, I'll see to it that you get the opportunity. That is, if the High Government permits further hopper operations, now that we've taken Lanoy into custody."

"I'll think about it," said Helaine quietly. "I don't know what I'll do. Just let me alone now. Thanks for everything, anyway, Joe."

She opaqued the screen and broke the contact. Now that the worst had happened, Helaine felt oddly calm. Glacially calm. She would not go into the past hunting for her husband. She was the widow Pomrath, betrayed, abandoned.

Joseph said, "Mommy, where's Daddy?"

"He's gone away, son."

"Will he be coming back soon?"

"I don't think so," Helaine said.

Marina looked up. "Does that mean that Daddy's dead?"

"Not quite," Helaine told her. "It's too complicated. I'll explain it some other time. Plug yourselves in and do your homework, children. It's almost bedtime."

She went to the drawer where they kept the alcohol tubes. Withdrawing one quickly, she pressed the snout against her skin and took a quick, subcutaneous jolt. It left her feeling neither more animated nor more depressed. She was frozen, at an emotional constant of zero.

The widow Pomrath. Beth Wisnack will be pleased to hear it. She can't bear the thought that any other woman might still have a husband.

Closing her eyes, she pictured Norm landing in 2050, a stranger and alone. He would make out, she knew. He had his medical skills. Dropped into the primitive past like that, he'd set up in business as a doctor, perhaps even

125

concealing his hopper status—otherwise he'd have been on the roster of registered hoppers, wouldn't he? He'd be rich and successful. Patients would flock to him, especially women patients. He would lose his look of bleak defeat, and take on the glow of prosperity. He'd stand taller, and smile more often. Helaine wondered what sort of woman he would marry. *Had* married. It was all done. That was the weird part of it. Norm had already lived and died, perishing about the year 2100, and his body had turned to dust centuries ago, along with the bodies of his other wife and his other children. Perhaps his descendants in today's world were a numerous tribe. Perhaps I'm one of them myself, Helaine thought. And the book was sealed; his destiny had been written hundreds of years before their wedding day. Even then, it was fated that he would leave her and circle back into the past to die hundreds of years before he was born.

Helaine's mind reeled. She took a second alcohol tube, and it helped her, but not much. The children sat with their backs to her, plugged into their homework machine, assiduously pretending to study.

I am lost, she thought.

I am nothing.

I am the widow Pomrath.

On the third tube, a new thought occurred to her. I am fairly young. Given a few months to relax, I could even be attractive again. Joe can arrange it; there must be a special government pension for the deserted wives of hoppers. I'll go away, fill out, put some meat on my bones. Then I'll marry again. Of course, I'll have used up my reproductive quota, but that won't matter. I can find a man who's willing to forego fatherhood. He'll adopt Joseph and Marina. Someone tall and handsome, and high in slope. Can I catch a Class Six? A widower, maybe even a man whose wife turned hopper, if there are any.

I'll show Norm. I'll catch myself a real prize.

Already, she could feel her body blossoming, filling out, the sap rising in it. For months, years even, she had lived in a barren winter of terror, clinging to her husband and nurturing him through his mood of empty despair in the hope that she could prevent him from abandoning her. Now that he was gone, she no longer needed to fear that he would go. She was returning to life. She felt younger.

I'll fix Norm Pomrath, Helaine thought. I'll make him sorry he ever went away!

thirteen

It was morning. Quellen had deliberately allowed the captured slyster Lanoy to languish overnight in the custody tank, so that he could reflect on his crimes. Lanoy was in total sensory deprivation, floating in a warm bath of nutrients with all inputs plugged off, so that nothing would register on his mind but his own predicament. Such treatment often had a marked softening effect on the hardest of cases. And from what Brogg had said, Lanoy was the hardest case in a long while.

Quellen had received the news at home, late in the evening, not long before Helaine's call. He had given instructions for Lanoy's treatment, but he had not actually gone down to headquarters to view the slyster. Leeward had brought him in, Brogg remaining behind at the hopper place itself.

It had been a somber night for Quellen. He knew, of course, that Norm Pomrath had gone to the past. He had been listening helplessly, jacked into the realtime circuit, while Pomrath and Lanoy discussed the project and came to an agreement. Then and there, Pomrath had paid over his money—virtually wiping out the family savings—and had stepped up on the platform to be thrust into the year 2050. Ear transmissions had ceased at that point. The Ear was a sensitive device, but it had no way of broadcasting across a temporal gap.

Helaine's stony face had been unpleasant to behold. She blamed him for what had happened, Quellen knew; and she never would really forgive him. So his sister, his only relative, was lost to him. And Judith, too, was lost. Since the fiasco at the social regurgitation communion, she had refused to take any calls from him. He knew that he would never see her again. The slender bare form in the sprayon costume postured wantonly in Quellen's dreams, waking him often.

The only comfort in a generally bleak situation was the fact that Lanoy had been found and arrested. That meant the heat would be off the department soon. With the hopper ring smashed, life could revert to routine, and Quellen would be free to spend most of his time in Africa, once again. Unless, of course, Brogg had really betrayed him. Quellen had forgotten about that. Koll's unfriendly tone of yesterday—did it mean that his own arrest was in the offing, as soon as the Lanoy affair was wrapped up?

Quellen got his answer to that shortly before midnight, when Koll called. For Koll, office hours extended throughout the night and the day.

"I've just checked with the office," Koll said. "They tell me you've got the slyster."

"Yes. He was brought in around eighteen, nineteen this evening. Brogg and Leeward traced him. They've put him in the custody tank. I'll interrogate him in the morning."

"Good job," Koll said, and Quellen noticed the trace of an honest smile flickering on the small man's lips. "This keys nicely into the status meeting Spanner and I had this afternoon. I've just put through a promotion form for you. It seems unfair to let the CrimeSec live in a Class Seven unit when he rates at least a Six, don't you think? You'll be joining Spanner and me in your higher grade quite soon. Of course, that won't affect your slope in the office hierarchy, but I thought you'd be pleased."

Quellen was pleased. And relieved. *So he doesn't know about Africa after all. It was just my guilty conscience stirring up fears.* Then a new worry came: how could he move the illegal stat to new quarters without being detected? It had been hard enough to get it installed here. Perhaps Koll was only leading him deeper into a trap. Quellen pressed his palms against his temples and shivered, waiting for morning—and Lanoy.

"You admit you've been sending people into the past?" Quellen demanded.

"Sure said the little man flippantly. Quellen stared at him, feeling an irrational pulse of anger throbbing in his skull. How could the slyster be so calm? "Sure," Lanoy said. "I'll send you back for two hundred units."

Leeward stood massively behind the little man, and Quellen faced him over the interrogation table. Brogg had not appeared at the office this morning. Koll and Spanner were listening from their own office next door. The slyster looked waxen-faced and limp from his night in the custody tank, and yet he held himself with dignity.

"You're Lanoy?" Quellen jabbed.

"That's my name." He was a small, dark, intense, rabbity sort of man, with thin lips constantly moving. "Sure, I'm Lanoy." The little slyster radiated a confident warmth. He was gaining strength from moment to moment. Now he sat with his legs crossed and his head thrown back.

"It was pretty nasty the way your boys tracked me down," Lanoy said. "It was bad enough that you fooled that poor dumb prolet into leading you to me, but you didn't have to dump me in the tank like that. I spent a lousy night. I'm not doing anything illegal, you know. I ought to sue."

"Nothing illegal? You're disturbing the past five hundred years!"

"I am not," Lanoy said calmly. "Nothing of the sort. They've already been disturbed. It's a matter of record, you know. I'm just seeing to it that past history gets to take place the way it took place, if you follow what I'm saying. I'm a public benefactor. What if I weren't fulfilling the records?"

Quellen glowered at the arrogant slyster. He turned to pace, found that he had no room to move in the tiny office, and sat down ineffectually at his desk. He felt strangely weak in the presence of the slyster. The man had power. Quellen said, "You admit that you're sending prolets back as hoppers. Why?"

Lanoy smiled. "To earn a living. Surely you understand that. I'm in possession of a very valuable process, and I want to make sure I get all I can out of it."

"Are you the inventor of the time-travel process?"

"I don't claim to be. But it doesn't matter," said Lanoy. "I control it."

"If you want to exploit your machine for money, why don't you simply go back in time and steal, or place bets on the arthropods, to make a living? Grab a quick killing on the outcome of a race that's in the records, then come back here."

"I could do that," Lanoy admitted. "But the process is

129

irreversible, and there's no way of getting back to the present again with my winnings. Or my stealings. And I like it here, thank you."

Quellen scratched his head. He *liked* it here? It seemed incredible that anyone would, but apparently Lanoy meant just what he said. One of those perverse estheticians, undoubtedly, who could find beauty in a dunghill.

He said, "Look, Lanoy, I'll be extremely frank with you: you're subject to penalties for operating this enterprise without the consent of the High Government. Kloofman has ordered your arrest. I'm not prepared to say what sort of a sentence you'll get, but it could be anything up to complete personality erasure, depending on your attitude. However, there's one option for you. The High Government wants control of your time-travel gimmick. Turn it over to my men—not just the device, you understand, but the method. Your cooperation will win you a remission of your sentence to some degree."

"Sorry," said Lanoy. "The machine's private property. You haven't got any right to it."

"The courts—"

"I'm not doing anything illegal, and so I don't need to worry about what kind of sentence I'll get. And I refuse to yield to your jurisdiction. The answer's no."

Quellen thought of the pressures that were on him from Koll and Spanner and even Kloofman to solve this case, and he got angry and frightened at the same time. He blurted, "When I get through with you, Lanoy, you'll wish you'd used your own machine and gone back a million years. We can induce cooperation. We can reduce you to jelly."

Lanoy's cool smile did not waver. His voice was measured as he said, "Come now, CrimeSec. You're starting to lose your temper, and that's always illogical. Not to add dangerous."

Quellen sensed the truth of Lanoy's warning. He struggled to calm himself, and lost the struggle. The muscles of his throat seemed to be writhing in knots. "I'll keep you in the tank until you rot," he snapped.

"Now where will that get you? I'll be so much moldy flesh, and you still won't be able to deliver the time process to the High Government." The slyster shrugged. "Would you mind giving me a little more oxy in here, please, by the way? I happen to be suffocating."

In his astonishment at the bold request, Quellen opened

the vent wide. Leeward registered surprise at Lanoy's breach of taste. No doubt the watchers in the next room were startled at Quellen's abrupt capitulation, too.

Lanoy said, "If you arrest me, I'll break you, Quellen. I tell you there's nothing illegal in what I'm doing. Look here—I'm a registered slyster." Lanoy produced a card, properly stamped.

Quellen was stymied. Lanoy definitely had him off balance. Ordinarily, he was better equipped to deal with criminals, but the events of the last few trying days had weakened his fibers. Quellen chewed his lip, watched the little man closely, and fervently wished that he were back beside his Congo stream throwing rocks at the crocodiles.

"I'm going to put a stop to your time-travel business, anyway," Quellen finally said.

Lanoy chuckled. "I wouldn't advise trying it, Quellen."

"CrimeSec to you."

"I wouldn't advise making trouble for me, *Quellen*," Lanoy repeated. "If you cut off the flow of the hoppers now, you'll turn the past topsy-turvy. Those people went back. It's recorded in history. Some of them married and had children, and the descendants of those children are alive today."

"I know all that. We've discussed the theory in great detail."

"For all you know, Quellen, you may be the descendant of a hopper I'm scheduled to be sending back next week— and if that hopper never gets back, Quellen, you'll pop out of existence like a snuffed candle. I guess it's a pleasant way to die. But do you want to die?"

Quellen stared glumly. Lanoy's words chased round and round in his aching skull. It became apparent to him now that it was a plot to drive him insane. Marok, Koll, Spanner, Brogg, Judith, Helaine, and now Lanoy—they were all determined to see Quellen enmeshed. It was an unvoiced conspiracy. Silently he cursed the hundreds of millions of jostling inhabitants of Appalachia, and wondered if he would ever know a moment's solitude again.

He took a deep breath. "The past won't be changed, Lanoy. We'll lock you up, all right, and take away your machine, but we'll see to it ourselves that the hoppers go back. We're not fools, Lanoy. We'll see to it that everything goes as it's supposed to go."

Lanoy watched him almost with pity for a moment, as

131

one might observe a particularly rare butterfly impaled on a mounting board.

"Is that your game, CrimeSec? Do you really think you'll learn to operate the machine?"

"I'm sure of it."

"In that case, I'll have to take steps to protect myself."

Quellen felt like hiding. "What could you possibly do?"

"You'll see. Suppose you put me back in the custody tank for the time being, while you figure out your own set of options. Then come and get me and talk to me again. Privately. I've got some interesting things to tell you. You won't want anyone else to hear them, though."

An aperture yawned in the sky, as though a quick hand had unzipped it. Norm Pomrath dropped through. His stomach protested as he made a rapid descent, falling eight or nine feet without warning. Lanoy might have told me, he thought, that I'd come out in the middle of the air. At the last moment he twisted and landed on his hip and his left leg. His kneecap tapped the pavement. Pomrath gasped and lay in a huddled heap for a moment, throbbing where he had bruised himself.

It wouldn't do to lie here long, he knew. He pulled himself together and got unsteadily to his feet, brushing himself off. The street was remarkably filthy. Pomrath's entire left side ached. He hobbled up against the wall of a building, clinging to it for a moment, and, clenching his teeth, performed one of the suggested neural exercises for enhancing the flow of blood. The pain began to ebb from him as the capillaries he had crushed emptied out.

There. That was better. He'd ache for a few hours, but it wasn't serious.

Now he had his first chance to look about him at the world of A.D. 2050.

He wasn't impressed. The city looked cluttered, as it would look four and a half centuries hence, but the clutter was a random, asymmetrical thing. Spiky buildings in an archaic style stuck up everywhere. There were no quickboat ramps and no bridges above the street levels. The pavement was cracked. The streets were crowded with pedestrians, not noticeably fewer than he was accustomed to seeing on the streets, although he knew that world population was only a third of what it would be in his rightful era. The styles of clothing interested him. Although it was springtime and the air was warm, everyone was dressed for maximum concealment, the women bundled up from ankles to chin, the men affecting loose capes that blurred the outlines of their body. So Pomrath knew that Lanoy had sent him approximately to the right time.

Pomrath had done some homework. He knew that the middle of the twenty-first century had been a time of neopuritan reaction against the fleshly excesses of the immediate past. He liked that. Nothing bored him more than an epoch of brazenly bare-breasted women and men in codpieces. True sensuality, he knew, thrived only in an era of erotic repression. Sensuality was one of the things he was looking for. After a decade as devoted father and faithful husband, Pomrath anticipated a fling.

He also knew that the neopuritan phase was soon to be struck down by another swing of the pendulum. So he would have the best of both cultures: first the covert pleasures of the inner revolt against the public morality, and then, in his declining days, the joys of witnessing the total breakdown of that morality. He had picked a good time. No wars to speak of, no particular crises. A man could enjoy himself here. Especially if he had useful skills, and a medical technician like Pomrath would thrive in this time of primitive medicine.

No one had seen him appear. At least, any witnesses to his materialization had quickly scurried on about their businesses, without meddling. Good.

He had to get his bearings, now.

He was in a city, presumably New York. Shops and offices all around. Pomrath drifted with the pedestrian tide. A kiosk at the corner was peddling what seemed to be the this-time equivalent of a faxtape. Pomrath stared. There was a date: May 6, 2051. Good old Lanoy. Within a year of the requested time. The yellow tape chuttered out of the slot in the machine. Pomrath had difficulty reading the ancient sans-serif type face. He hadn't realized how the shapes of the letters had changed. A moment though, and he had the hang of it.

Fine. Now all he needed was some money, an identity, a place to live. Within a week, he felt, he would be fully established in the matrix of this era.

He filled his lungs with air. He felt confident, bouncy, buoyant. There was no job machine here. He could live by

133

his own wits, doing solitary battle with the inexorable forces of the universe and actually getting the universe to yield a little. In his own time, he was just a number on a punched card, a patch of ions on a coded tape. Here he was free to select his own role and capitalize on it.

Pomrath stepped into a shop at random. They were selling books in there. Not spools; *books*. He looked at them in wonder. Cheap, sleazy paper; blurry ink; flimsy bindings. He picked up a novel, flipped its pages, put it down. He found what seemed to be a popular medical guide. It would be useful; Pomrath wondered how he could gain possession of it without money. He didn't want to admit to anyone that he was a hopper. He wanted to make the grade by his own devices.

A man whom he assumed was the proprietor came up to him—plump, grimy-faced, with watery blue eyes. Pomrath smiled. He knew that his clothing marked him as a stranger, but he hoped it didn't stamp him too clearly as a stranger out of time.

The man said in a soft, feathery voice, "There's better downstairs. Want to catch some haunch?"

Pomrath's smile grew broader. "Sorry, I be not easy speaking. My English very hard."

"Haunch, I said. *Haunch*. Downstairs. You from out of town?"

"Visitor from Slavic country. Incomplete grasp your language," Pomrath said, laying on what he hoped sounded like a thick Czech accent. "Maybe you help? Am feeling unsettled here."

"That's what I thought. A lonely foreigner. Well, go downstairs. The girls'll cheer you up. Twenty dollars. You got dollars?"

Pomrath began to see what was going on in the basement of the bookshop. He nodded vociferously and headed toward the rear of the store, still clutching his medical guide. The proprietor didn't appear to notice that he had taken the book.

Stairs led below. Stairs! Pomrath hardly knew what they were. He gripped the railing tightly, unsure of his footing as he descended. At the bottom, some sort of scanner beamed him and he heard a blipping sound that probably indicated he was carrying no weapons. A fleshy woman in bulky robes came swishing out to inspect him.

In his own time there were public sex cubicles available

to all, without concealment. It figured that in this neopuritan era there would be girlie cribs hidden in the lower levels of musty old buildings. Vice, Pomrath thought, was probably more common here per capita than up yonder.

The woman said, "You're the foreigner Al said was coming down, huh? You sure look foreign to me. Where you from, France?"

"Slavic district. Praha."

"Where's that?"

Pomrath looked uncertain. "Europe. To the east."

The woman shrugged and led him with. Pomrath found himself in a small, low-ceilinged room which contained a bed, a washstand, and a pasty-faced blonde girl. The girl slipped off her robe. Her body was soft and slightly flabby, but the basic material was pretty good. She looked young and more intelligent than her job called on her to be.

"It's twenty dollars," she said patiently.

Pomrath knew that the moment of truth had arrived. He flicked a wary glance around the little room and saw no sign of any scanning devices. He couldn't be sure, naturally. Even way back here, they had been pretty sophisticated about espionage, and he didn't doubt that they pulled the same dirty tricks that were common in his own time. But he had to take the risk. Sooner or later, he had to find himself an ally in this other time, and now was a reasonable time to begin.

"I don't have any money," said Pomrath, dropping the phony accent.

"Then get the hell out of here."

"Shh. Not so fast. I've got some ideas. Sit down. Relax. How would you like to be rich?"

"Are you a cop?"

"I'm just a stranger in town, and I need a friend. I've got plans. Cooperate with me and you'll be out of the bed-girl business in a hurry. What's your name?"

"Lisa. You talk funny. What are you, a hopper or something?"

"Is it that obvious?"

"Just a guess." The girl's eyes were very blue, very wide. She picked up her robe and put it on again, as though she did not think it proper to hold a business conference in the nude. She kept her voice low as she said, "You just get here?"

"Yes. I'm a doctor. I can make us fabulously rich. With what I know—"

"We'll turn all the turbines, child!" she said. "You and me. What's your label?"

"Keystone," Pomrath said at random. "Mort Keystone."

"We're going to twist orbits, Mort."

"I know we are. How soon can you get out of this place?"

"Two more hours."

"Where should I meet you?"

"There's a park two blocks from here. You can sit there and wait and I'll come along."

"A what?"

"A park. You know, grass, benches, some trees. What's the matter, Mort?"

Pomrath was struck by the alienness of having trees and grass in the middle of a city. He managed a smile. "Nothing's the matter. I'll wait for you in the park." Then he handed her the book. "Here. Buy this for me when you leave the shop. I don't want to have to steal it."

She nodded. Then she said, "You sure you don't want anything else while you're down here?"

"There's time for that later," said Pomrath. "I'll be waiting in the park."

He went out. The bookstore proprietor waved cheerily to him. Pomrath replied in a string of improvised guttural sounds and stepped into the street. It was difficult for him to believe that he had been on the verge of psychotic collapse only a few hours ago and four hundred forty-nine years from now. He was utterly calm. This world held challenges for him, and he knew he could meet those challenges.

Poor Helaine, he thought. I wonder how she took the news.

He walked briskly down the street, only momentarily bothered by the lack of resilience in the pavement. I am Mort Keystone, he told himself. Mort Keystone. Mort Keystone. And Lisa will help me get together some money to start a medical practice. I'll be a rich man. I'll live like A Class Two. There's no High Government to slap me down.

I'll have power and status among these primitives, he

136

told himself pleasantly. And after I'm established, I'll track down a few people from my own time, just so I don't feel too isolated from it. We'll reminisce, he thought.

We'll reminisce about the future.

fourteen

Quellen waited three hours, until Koll and Spanner both were tied up on other government business. Then he went down the hall to the custody tank. He opened the scanner slot and peered in. Lanoy floated peacefully on the dark green fluid, utterly relaxed, evidently enjoying himself. On the stippled metal wall of the tank the indicators announced the slyster's status. EEG and EKG bands wavered and criss-crossed. Heartbeat, respiration, everything was monitored.

Summoning a technician, Quellen said, "Get him out of there."

"Sir, we just put him back in a few hours ago."

"I want to interrogate him. Get him out!"

The technician obeyed. Lanoy was unplugged, filtered, and returned to consciousness. Attendant-robots wheeled him back to Quellen's office. In a short while his reflexes were working again and he could move under his own power.

Quellen shut down all recording devices in the office. He had a strong hunch that he wanted this conversation to be strictly off the record. Since there were only the two of them in the room, he also moved to cut down the oxy vent.

"Leave it up, Quellen," Lanoy said. "I like to breathe well. It's at government expense."

"Let's finish our talk, then. What's your game?" Quellen was angry. Lanoy was a completely amoral creature, not even vicious in his criminality, who offended Quellen's pride and sense of personal dignity.

"I'll be blunt with you, CrimeSec," the slyster said. "I want my freedom, and I want to continue in business. I

138

like it that way. That's what *I* want. You want to arrest me and let the government or perhaps the High Government take over my business. That's what *you* want. Right?"

"Right."

"Now in a situation like that we have an interplay of mutually exclusive desires. So the stronger of the two forces wins—all the time. I'm stronger, and so you'll have to let me go and suppress all the findings of your investigation."

"Who says you're stronger, Lanoy?"

"I know I am. I'm strong and you're weak. I know a lot of things about you, Quellen. I know how you hate crowds and like fresh air and open spaces. These are pretty awkward idiosyncrasies to live with in a world like ours, aren't they?"

"Go on," said Quellen. He cursed Brogg silently. No one else could have revealed his secret to Lanoy. And obviously Lanoy knew too much about him.

"So you're going to let me walk out of here a free man," Lanoy continued, "or else you'll find yourself back in a Class Nine or maybe Eleven unit. You won't like it much there, CrimeSec. You'll have to share a room, and you may not like your roommate, but there'll be nothing you can do. And when you have a roommate, you won't be free to run away. He'll report you."

"What do you mean, run away?" Quellen's voice was little more than a husky whisper.

"I mean run away to Africa, Quellen."

That's it, then, Quellen thought. Now it's over; Brogg's sold me completely down the river. He knew that with Lanoy in possession of the secret, he was totally in the little slyster's power. He stood motionless before Lanoy, seething with the temptation to grab up a televector cable and knot it fatally around Lanoy's neck.

Lanoy said, "I hate to do this to you, Quellen. Actually. There's no personal animus in it at all. You're a pretty good sort, caught in a world you didn't make and don't especially like. But I can't help myself. It's either you or me, and you know who's got to win in a deal like that."

"How did you find out?"

"Brogg told me."

"Why would he do a thing like that? He was getting a good price from me."

"I gave him a better one," said Lanoy. "I sent him back

to Hadrian's time. Possibly Trajan. He's gone back 2400 years, at any rate."

Quellen felt the floor turn to sticky rubber beneath his feet, writhing and squirming and pulsing with heat. He clung to his desk so he would not slide through into oblivion. Brogg a hopper! Brogg gone? Brogg a traitor?

"When did this happen?" Quellen asked.

"Yesterday evening, about sunset. Brogg and I discussed the problem of how I was going to avoid being put out of business. He suggested that you had a point of vulnerability. I got it from him in return for the one thing he really wanted. He's gone back to see Rome with his own eyes."

"That's impossible," Quellen insisted. "There are records on the known hoppers, and Brogg wasn't on the list."

Even as he spoke, he knew how foolish the words were. The records went back only to A.D. 1979. Brogg—unless Lanoy were bluffing—was almost nineteen centuries further back. There'd be no record.

Quellen felt sick. He knew that Brogg had planted autonomic telltales all over Appalachia, with taped accounts of Quellen's crime in them. The telltales were programmed to march down to headquarters in the event of Brogg's death or disappearance. The little springy legs must have been in motion since last night. I'm finished Quellen thought. Unless Brogg had the good grace to deactivate the telltales before he hopped. He could have done it with no great trouble. The boxes responded to telephoned instruction. One call would have shut them down. But had he? Otherwise, the High Government was even now in possession of the truth about Joseph Quellen.

Quellen had talked to Koll only this morning, though, and Koll had congratulated him on his promotion. Koll was guileful, but not to that degree. He would surely have been the recipient of one of Brogg's little telltales, and he wouldn't have been able to conceal his fury and envy at the discovery that Quellen had been living in Class Two luxury all this time.

So possibly Brogg had turned the telltales off. Or possibly he had never gone hopper at all.

Scowling, Quellen slammed on his communicator and said, "Get me Brogg."

"I'm sorry, UnderSec Brogg hasn't been in contact today."

"Not even to give a locus notice?"

"We haven't heard from him, sir."

140

"Ring his apartment. Check the district headquarters. If there's no word from him within the next fifteen minutes, initiate a televector search. I want to know where he is!"

Lanoy was beaming. "You're not going to find him, Quellen. Believe me, he's in Rome. I set up the displacement myself—temporal and geographical. If everything worked out, he landed just south of the city, somewhere along the Via Appia."

Quellen's lips twitched. He was gripping the desk very, very tightly, now, so that his fingertips were beginning to make indentations in the top, which was thermal-sensitive and not designed to be handled that way. He said, "If you can send somebody back that far in time, how is it that 1979 has been the terminal date for the hopper phenomenon?"

"Lots of reasons."

"Such as?"

"For one, the process wasn't reliable beyond about five hundred years until recently. We've improved the process. New research. Now we can confidently shoot people back a couple of thousand years and know they'll get there."

"The pigs in the twelfth century?"

"Yes," Lanoy said. "Those were our experimental shots. Now, then: it also happens that such a concentration of hoppers got sent back to the 1979 nexus that the phenomenon came to the attention of authorities. Any hopper landing in a previous *elsewhen* would generally end up detained for insanity, or arrested for witchcraft, or something. So we tried to limit our hoppers to the 1979 to 2106 period because any hopper landing there would be recognized for what he was, and he'd have minimal troubles. We only exceeded that range upon special request, or sometimes by an unintentional overshoot. You follow?"

"Yes," said Quellen glumly. "And Brogg went back to Rome?"

"He really did. For a price. And now you'd better let me go, promising to keep the results of your investigation from getting any higher, or I'll expose your little game. I'll let it be known that you've got a hideaway in Africa."

Quellen said coolly, "I could put a beam through your head right now and claim that you assaulted me."

"No good, Quellen. For one thing, the High Government wants the time-transport process. Kill me and you lose the process."

"We could dredge it out of your brain on a neural replay dead or alive."

"Not if you lase me through the head," Lanoy pointed out. "Anyway, the neural replay would also dredge up the Africa bit, wouldn't it? Beside that, you'd suffer if I died. Didn't you know that Brogg fed your story into a bunch of autonomic telltales programmed to walk into government headquarters if anything happened to him?"

"Yes, but—"

"He keyed them all over to me just before he hopped. Your fate is tied to mine, Quellen. You don't want to harm me. You want to let me go."

Quellen could feel the muscles of his face sag as the nastiness of his position came home. If he did not present Lanoy for prosecution, he ran the risk of demotion. If he turned Lanoy in, Lanoy would expose him. Nor could he simply let Lanoy walk out the way the slyster wished. It was already a matter of record that Lanoy was involved in the hopper affair. Koll knew. Spanner knew. Quellen could not easily expunge the knowledge from the records. If he tried to cover up for Lanoy, he would mire himself in lie upon lie. He was living one fraud as it was; he could not bear the strain of assuming another.

"Do I get what I want?" Lanoy asked.

A powerful surge of adrenalin rocked through Quellen. He was a man in a trap, and a trapped man fights fiercely. He found unexpected reserves of strength.

There was one thing he could try, a monumentally audacious thing, something so vastly bold that it seemed almost sensible in its way. Perhaps it would fail; probably it would fail. But it was better than making deals with Lanoy and slipping deeper into a morass of bribery and compromise.

"No," he said. "You don't get what you want. I'm not releasing you, Lanoy. I'm going to remand you for indictment."

"Are you crazy?"

"I don't think so." Quellen rang for attendants. "Put this man back in the custody tank," he said crisply. "Leave him there until further notice."

Lanoy was carried away, sputtering and protesting.

Now to secure the bait for the leviathan he hoped to share.

Quellen jabbed communicator buttons. "Get me the Donald Mortensen file," he commanded.

The spool was brought to him. He threaded it through the projector and looked over Brogg's investigation. The face of Mortensen gleamed out at him, youthful, pink. He looked like some kind of albino, Quellen thought, with that white hair and eyebrows. But albinos have pink eyes, don't they? Mortensen's were blue. Pure Nordic. How had he preserved his bloodline so well, Quellen wondered? He examined Mortensen's dossier.

Quellen pored over the recorded texts of Brogg's pickups. Mortensen had quarreled with his wife; he had negotiated for a hopper trip several weeks hence; he had put money down, and was busily raising the rest of Lanoy's fee. Then the data ended with Brogg's notation: INVESTIGATION CONCLUDED BY OFFICIAL ORDER.

Quellen rang the listening room. He gave the number of the Ear that had been pressed into Mortensen's palm and asked if it was still functioning.

"The Ear's been deactivated, CrimeSec," he was told.

"Yes, I know. But can it be turned on again?"

They checked. A few minutes later they gave him the bad news; the Ear had dissolved a day or two ago, as it was designed to do. There were no further transmissions from Mortensen. Quellen was disappointed, but the setback was not critical. He ordered a televector check on Mortensen's whereabouts, hoping fiercely that he had not gone out of Appalachia.

He hadn't. The televector tracer reported that Mortensen was in a sniffer palace less than ten miles from Quellen's office. Excellent, Quellen thought. He would make the arrest himself. This was something far too delicate to leave it to a subordinate.

Catching a quickboat, Quellen crossed the city and stationed himself outside the sniffer palace, waiting on street level for Mortensen to come up from the depths. Seamy, shifty-eyed individuals kept shuttling past him. Quellen masked his discomfort and scanned everyone who emerged.

There was Mortensen now.

It was a long time since Quellen had made an arrest in person. He was a desk man, who left such contacts to underlings. Nevertheless he felt calm. He was well armed; taped to the palm of his hand was an anesthetic prong that would flip out at a command of his muscles, and beneath his armpit was a neural spray in case something went awry with the prong. He carried a laser pistol too, but the last thing he intended was to use it on Mortensen.

Moving in behind the man as he strode away from the sniffer palace, Quellen tapped him on the shoulder and said, "Just keep walking calmly, Mortensen. You're under arrest."

"What the hell—?"

"I'm from the Secretariat of Crime. I've got orders to bring you in. There's a prong in my palm and I'll slap it into you in a hurry if you attempt to resist. Walk quietly ahead of me until we get to that quickboat ramp. You do as I say and you won't get into trouble."

"I haven't done anything wrong. I want to know the charge."

"Later," said Quellen. "Keep walking."

"I have legal rights. A lawyer—"

"Later. Walk."

They ascended the flyramp. Mortensen continued to grumble, but he made no show of resistance. He was a tall man, taller than Quellen. He did not look particularly powerful, though. Quellen kept his prong-laden palm ready. His entire future depended on the successful completion of this maneuver.

The quickboat took them to Quellen's apartment building.

Mortensen looked puzzled. As they stepped out on the ramp, he grunted sullenly, "This doesn't look like a crime office to me."

"Down the ramp, please," Quellen said.

"What is this, a kidnapping?"

"I'll show you my credentials if you're worried. I'm an authentic peace officer. As a matter of fact, I hold the rank of CrimeSec. Step in here."

They entered Quellen's apartment. Mortensen, facing Quellen, stared at him incredulously.

"This is a private residence," he said.

"True. Mine."

"Somebody's clearly given you the wrong tip on my sexual orientation, friend. I'm not—"

"Neither am I," said Quellen sharply. "Mortensen, are you planning to go hopper the first week in May?"

Glaring, Mortensen said, "What's that to you?"

"A good deal. Is it true?"

"Maybe. I'm not saying."

Quellen sighed. "You're on the list of hoppers who went

144

back, do you know that? A fully documented list giving your name, your date of birth, the day you arrived in the past, the day you left here. The list says you went back on May 4 of this year. Now do you want to deny that you're planning to hop?"

"I'm not saying anything. Get me a lawyer. Damn you, I didn't threaten you in any way! Why did you have to muck around with my life?"

"I can't explain that now," said Quellen. "It happens that you're the unfortunate victim of a situation that's getting out of hand. Mortensen, I'm going to send you on a journey. You're going to have a vacation. I can't say how long you'll be away, but at least you'll be comfortable there. You'll find a full food program; help yourself. And rest assured that I'll be looking out for your welfare. I'm on your side, actually. Deeply sympathetic to your position. But I've got to look out for myself, first."

The troubled Mortensen lifted a hand as though to lash out at Quellen. Smoothly, Quellen moved forward and activated the anesthetic prong on his hand. It bit into Mortensen's skin. The instantaneous anesthetic went to work, and Mortensen folded up into unconsciousness. He would be out for about an hour, which was more than enough time.

Quellen turned on the stat field and shoved Mortensen through. The blond man vanished. He would wake up in the CrimeSec's African cottage. No doubt that would add to his general bafflement, but Quellen had not been able to offer explanations.

A moment later the stat was turned off at Quellen's end. That would keep Mortensen from getting back until Quellen was ready to bring him back.

Waves of vertigo swept through him.

He had the bait. Now he had to play his fish. It seemed incredible that he would succeed, but he had gone too far to permit himself to turn back. And, if he failed, he was beginning to see, there was an alternative way out, less honorable but possibly more rational a solution than what he had in mind.

Can I get away with this, he wondered? Can I actually try to blackmail the High Government and make it stick? Or am I simply out of my mind altogether?

He would find that out soon enough. Meanwhile, he had a hostage—Mortensen. A hostage against the wrath of the High Government.

Now, just one small thing remained: to get an interview with Peter Kloofman. Himself. In person. Could it be arranged? It was a staggering dream. How could a Class Seven bureaucrat gain admission to the presence of Kloofman?

He'll see me, Quellen thought. When he learns that I've kidnapped Donald Mortensen.

fifteen

David Giacomin, who had been carrying out some quiet monitoring of the Mortensen situation himself, was the first to discover that there was trouble. A flashing red light informed him that Mortensen had vanished from the reach of the Appalachia televector field.

Giacomin experienced a sensation of disorientation. The critical day for Mortensen was May 4; and May 4 was still several weeks off. It wasn't possible for him to have gone hopper so soon, was it?

Yes, it *was* possible, Giacomin reflected. But if he had, why hadn't the fabric of space and time tottered? The past had been altered—or else the records had been in error in the first place. Giacomin ordered a full investigation into the Mortensen disappearance to be carried out, mobilizing every resource of the High Government. Kloofman had personally instructed Giacomin to see that nothing happened to Mortensen; and now it appeared as though something had indeed happened. The perspiring Giacomin reflected that he had damned well get Mortensen back before Kloofman found out he was missing.

Then, almost simultaneously, Giacomin learned that he was going to have to break the news to Kloofman after all.

A call came through from Koll in the Secretariat of Crime, the ratty-faced little Class Six through whom Giacomin supervised that wing of governmental activities. Koll looked upset, even dazed. His face was flushed and his eyes were fixed and glossy.

"I've got someone here who wants an interview with

147

Kloofman," Koll said. "A Class Seven—no, he'll soon be Six—in my department."

"He's insane. Kloofman wouldn't see him, and you know it, so why are you bothering me with this?"

"He says he's kidnapped Mortensen, and he wants to discuss the situation with somebody in Class One."

Giacomin stiffened. His hands began to move in spasmodic jerks, and he fought to get them under control. "Who is this maniac?"

"Quellen. He's the CrimeSec here. He—"

"Yes, I know him. When did he make this request?"

"Ten minutes ago. First he tried to call Kloofman direct, but that didn't work. So now he's going through channels. He asked me and I'm asking you. What else can I do?"

"Nothing else, I suppose," said Giacomin hollowly. His quick mind sifted the possible things that could be done to the troublesome Quellen, beginning with slow disembowelment and proceeding from there. But Quellen had Mortensen, or said he did. And Kloofman was practically psychotic on the subject of Mortensen. He talked of little else.

There went Giacomin's carefully crafted plan to keep the news about Mortensen's disappearance from getting to the top man. He saw no way of avoiding that now. He could stall for time, but in the end Quellen would have his way.

"Well?" Koll said. The tip of his nose quivered. "Can I remand his request officially to your level?"

"Yes," Giacomin said. "I'll take it off your hands. Let me talk to Quellen."

A moment passed. Quellen appeared on the screen. He *looked* sane, Giacomin thought. A little frightened at his own audacity, no doubt, but generally rational. At least as rational as Koll, for that matter.

But determined. He wanted to see Kloofman. Yes, he had kidnapped Mortensen. No, he would not divulge the whereabouts of the kidnapped man. Moreover, any attempt to interfere with his freedom of action would result in the immediate death of Mortensen.

Was it a bluff? Giacomin didn't dare take the chance. He looked at Quellen in quiet wonder and said, "All right. You win, you madman. I'll pass your request for an audience along to Kloofman and we'll see what he says."

148

It was such a long time since Kloofman had consented to speak face to face with a member of the lower orders that he had nearly forgotten what the experience was like. He had some Class Threes and Fours and even Fives in attendance on him, of course, but they didn't converse with him. They could just as well have been robots. Kloofman tolerated no chitchat from such people. High on the lonely eminence of Class One, the world leader had cut himself off from contact with the masses.

He awaited the arrival of this person Quellen, then, with some curiosity. Resentment, of course; he was not accustomed to coercion. Anger. Irritation. Yet Kloofman was amused, as well. The pleasure of vulnerability had been denied him for many years. He could take a light approach to this unexpected crisis.

He was also frightened. So far as the televector men could tell, Quellen actually *did* have possession of Mortensen. That was distressing. It was a direct threat to Kloofman's power. He could not laugh at such a situation.

The subcranial probe murmured to Kloofman, "Quellen is here."

"Let him in."

The chamber wall rolled back. A lean, haggard-looking man walked awkwardly in and stood flatfooted before the huge pneumatic web in which Kloofman reposed. Between Kloofman and Quellen there rose a fine, almost imperceptible mist, an assassination screen extending from floor to ceiling. Any particle of solid matter attempting to cross that screen would be instantly volatilized, no matter what its mass or velocity. Robot wardens flanked Kloofman as an additional precaution. Kloofman waited patiently. The artificial systems within his reconstituted body purred smoothly, pumping blood through the vessels, bathing the inner meat with lymph. He saw that Quellen was uncomfortable in his presence. It scarcely surprised him.

At length Kloofman said, "You've had your wish. Here I am. What do you want?"

Quellen moved his lips, but there was a lag of several seconds before he produced words. "Do you know what I'm thinking?" he blurted finally. "I'm glad you exist. That's what I'm thinking. It's relieving to know that you're real."

Kloofman managed to smile. "How do you *know* I'm real?"

"Because—" Quellen stopped. "All right. I retract that.

149

I hope you're real." His hands were quivering at his sides. Kloofman observed the man make a visible effort to pull himself together—an effort that seemed to be at least outwardly successful.

"Are you the man who kidnapped Mortensen?"

"Yes."

"Where is he?"

"I can't reveal that, sir. Not yet. I've got to propose a deal with you first."

"A deal with *me?*" Kloofman delivered himself of a rumbling chuckle. "You're incredible in your brazenness," he said mildly. "Don't you realize what I can do to you?"

"Yes."

"And yet you come here to bargain with me?"

"I have Mortensen," Quellen reminded him. "Unless I release him, he won't be free to hop on May 4. And that means—"

"Yes," said Kloofman sharply. He felt tension levels climbing within his body. This man had found his zone of vulnerability, all right. It was preposterous that he should be held at bay by a prolet, but that was the situation. Kloofman could take no chances with a man who threatened to change the past. No computer simulation could possibly calculate the effects of subtracting the hopper Donald Mortensen from his proper time destination. The world leader was helpless. Kloofman said, "You're playing a dangerous game, Quellen. State your business. Then you'll be removed and the location of Mortensen will be dredged from your mind."

"Mortensen is programmed to destruct in the event of any tampering with my brain," said Quellen.

Could that be true, Kloofman wondered? Or was this all some gigantic bluff?

"Your business."

Quellen nodded. He seemed to be gaining poise and strength, as though he had discovered that Kloofman was no superbeing, but merely a very old man with great power. Quellen said, "I was assigned to the investigation into the time-travel operation. I've succeeded in finding the man who controls it. He's under arrest now. Unfortunately, he's in possession of information that incriminates me in an illegal act."

"Are you a criminal, Quellen?"

"I've done something illegal. It could bring me demotion and worse. If I turn the slyster over to your

150

people, he'll expose me. So I want immunity. That's the deal. I'll give you your man, and he'll blab about my crime, but you'll confirm me in my position and see to it that I'm not prosecuted or demoted."

"What's your crime, Quellen?"

"I maintain a Class Two villa in Africa."

Kloofman smiled. "You *are* a scoundrel, aren't you?" he said without rancor. "You connive out of your class, you blackmail the High Government—"

"Actually I regard myself as fairly honest, sir."

"I suppose you do. But you're a scoundrel all the same. Do you know what I'd do with a dangerous man like you, if I had my options? I'd put you in the time machine and hurl you far into the past. That's the safest way to deal with agitators. That's how we'll cope, once we—" Kloofman fell silent. After a moment he said, "Your boldness stupefies me. What if I lie to you? I grant you your immunity, you turn Mortensen over to me and surrender the time-travel slyster, and then I seize you and arrest you all the same."

"I have two other documented hoppers hidden away," said Quellen blandly. "One is due to depart later this year and the other one early next year. They're further insurance that you won't harm me after I've given you Mortensen."

"You're bluffing, Quellen. You've invented those other two hoppers on the spot. I'll put you under a neural probe and check on it."

"The moment the probe touches my brain," said Quellen, "Mortensen will die."

Kloofman felt unaccustomed anguish. He was certain that this infuriating prolet was piling bluff upon bluff—but there was no way of proving that without peering into his brain, and bluff number one made it too risky for Kloofman to try that. It might just not be a bluff.

He said, "What do you really want, Quellen?"

"I've told you. A pledge of immunity, before witnesses. I want you to guarantee that I won't be punished for maintaining my place in Africa, and that I'll come to no harm for having bearded you like this. Then I'll give you the slyster and Mortensen."

"And the other two hoppers."

"Those also. After I've become assured of your good faith."

"You're incredible, Quellen. But you seem to hold a

strong position. I can't let you keep Mortensen. And I want that time machine. It's got many uses for us. Profitable uses. Politically beneficial uses. Too dangerous to let it stay in private hands. All right. All right. You'll have your pledge. I'll give you more than that, Quellen."

"More, sir?"

"Your villa's Class Two, you say? I assume you want to go on living in it. We'll have to make you Class Two then, won't we?"

"Take me into the High Government, sir?"

"Of course," said Kloofman warmly. "Consider: how can I send you back to lower levels, after you've triumphed over me like this? You've won status. I'll put you up here. Giacomin will find room for you. A man who's done what you've done can't possibly remain in a low bureaucratic post, Quellen. So we'll arrange something. You've won more than you came looking for." Kloofman smiled. "I congratulate you, Quellen."

Quellen erupted into the upper air, after having risen level upon level upon level from that mythical catacomb that was the lair of Peter Kloofman. He staggered out into the street and planted himself solidly, feet on the pavement, head upturned to the towers far above. He saw the lacy connecting bridges, the gleaming cones atop the buildings, the faint patch of blue light beyond the summits.

I don't have much time, Quellen thought.

He was numb with shock after his interview with Kloofman. In retrospect he had no idea how he had carried off such an enterprise. To muscle his way into the lair of a Class One administrator, to stand there bluntly making demands and having Kloofman accede to them, to pile fraud upon fraud and carry his bluffs home—it was not real. It couldn't be. It had to be some sniffer palace fantasy, some dream of power that would fade with the ebbing of the drug from his brain.

Yet the buildings were real. The sky was real. The pavements were real. And the interview with Kloofman had been real, too. He had won. He had been invited to accept Class Two status. He had compelled Kloofman to retreat.

Quellen knew that he had not won a thing.

He had done his audacious maneuver with reasonable aplomb, but it had been a fool's maneuver, and he saw that more clearly now than he had an hour before. Any man could be proud of having had the nerve to confront Kloofman like that, but, having done it, Quellen knew that he had gained no real safety, only the temporary illusion of triumph. It would be necessary to activate the alternate plan that he had been nurturing for some hours. His mind had prepared itself for this eventuality, and he knew what he had to do, though he was not at all sure that he would have time to do it.

He was in mortal danger. He had to act fast.

Kloofman had not fooled him with his smiles, his words of praise, his promise of an uptwitch to High Government status, his apparent delight in Quellen's audacity. Kloofman was frightened that something might happen to Mortensen that could topple his own power, yes, but Kloofman could not be pushed around as easily as it seemed.

He'll get Lanoy and Mortensen from me, Quellen knew, and then he'll destroy me. I should have realized that from the start. How could I hope to outsmart Kloofman?

But he did not regret having made the attempt. A man is not a worm; he can stand up on his legs, he can fight for his position. He can try. Quellen had tried. He had done something foolhardy to the point of absurdity, and he had carried it off with honor, even if his success was probably unreal.

Now, though, he had to hasten to protect himself against Kloofman's wrath. He had at least a little time in which to operate. The euphoria of his meeting with Kloofman had worn off, and he was thinking clearly and rationally.

He reached the headquarters of the Secretariat of Crime and immediately gave orders for Lanoy to be taken from the custody tank once again. The slyster was brought to Quellen's office. He looked moody and downcast.

"You're going to be sorry for this, Quellen," Lanoy said bitterly. "I wasn't joking when I said Brogg had keyed all his telltales over to me. I can have the news of your African place in the hands of the High Government in—"

"You don't need to inform on me," said Quellen. "I'm letting you go."

Lanoy was startled. "But you said—"

"That was earlier. I'm releasing you and wiping out as much as I can of the records involving you."

"So you gave in after all, Quellen? You knew you couldn't take the risk that I'd expose you?"

"On the contrary. I haven't given in. I told the High Government about my African place myself. I let Kloofman himself know, in person. No sense wasting time talking to underlings. So your telltales won't be telling anything that isn't already known."

"You can't ask me to believe that, Quellen!"

"It's the truth, though. And therefore the price for my letting you go has changed. It isn't your silence any more. It's your services."

Lanoy's eyes widened. "What have you been up to?"

"Plenty. But there's no time for me to explain it now. I'll get you safely out of this building. You've got to get back to your lab on your own power. I'll join you there in about an hour." Quellen shook his head. "Not that I think you'll stay free for very long, Lanoy. Kloofman's hungry for your machine. He wants to use it to send political prisoners back. And to raise public revenues. He'll solve his unemployment problem by shooting the prolets back to 500,000 B.C. and letting them get eaten by tigers. You'll be picked up again, I'm sure of it. But at least it won't be my doing."

He escorted Lanoy from the building. The little slyster gave Quellen a baffled look as he scuttled away toward the quickboat ramp.

"I'll be seeing you in a little while," Quellen said.

He boarded a quickboat himself, a local, and headed for his apartment to perform one last chore. Had Kloofman taken steps against him yet? Doubtless They were having frantic conferences in the chambers of the High Government. It wouldn't be long now, though, and Quellen would be safe.

He had come to understand a great many things. Why Kloofman wanted the machine so badly, for one thing: as a tool to extend his own power over the world. Unscrupulous, it was. And I nearly helped him get it.

Then, too, Quellen saw why the recorded hoppers had all come from 2486-91. It didn't mean that the backward flow had been cut off next year, as he had assumed. It simply meant that control of the machine had passed then from Lanoy to Kloofman, and that all hoppers sent back after 2491 were hurled by the new process, which had a greater range, thrown back so far that they could be no possible threat to Kloofman's regime. And would not, of course, show up in any historical records. Quellen

154

shuddered. He wanted no part of a world in which the government held such powers.

He entered his apartment and activated the stat. The glow of theta force enveloped him. Quellen stepped through, and emerged in his African cottage.

"Mortensen?" he shouted. "Where are you?"

"Down here!"

Quellen peered over the edge of the porch. Mortensen was fishing. Stripped to the waist, his pale skin partly red and partly tan, he waved to Quellen affably.

"Come on," Quellen said. "You're going home!"

"I'd rather stay, thank you. I like it here."

"Nonsense. You've got a date to hop."

"Why hop if I can hang out here?" Mortensen asked reasonably. "I don't understand why you brought me here, but I don't feel like leaving now."

Quellen had no time to argue. It did not fit into his plan to keep Mortensen from making his May 4 hop. Quellen had no vested interest in disturbing the recorded past, and Mortensen's value as a hostage would shortly be zero. It was conceivable that Mortensen's failure to hop on schedule would jeopardize Quellen's own continued existence, if he happened to be a descendant of the hopped Mortensen. Why take the risk? Mortensen would have to hop.

"Come," Quellen said.

"No."

Sighing, Quellen moved in and once again anesthetized the man. He hauled the limp Mortensen into the cottage and thrust him through the stat, following a moment later himself. Mortensen lay sprawled out on the floor of Quellen's apartment. In a short while, he'd awaken and try to comprehend all that had been happening to him, and perhaps he'd attempt to get back to Africa. But by then he would have registered on the Appalachia televector field, and Kloofman's men would be on their way to pick him up. Kloofman would make sure that Mortensen hopped on schedule.

Quellen left the apartment for the last time. He ascended the flyramp and waited for the quickboat. He knew the route to Lanoy's place, thanks to Brogg.

He would rather have triumphed over Kloofman than have taken this route. But he had been in a trap, and a man in a trap must seek the sane path to freedom, not the most glamorous one. There was irony in the decision, of course: the man assigned to police the hopper problem becoming a hopper himself. Yet there was a kind of inevitability, Quellen saw, right from the start, that made him one with Norm Pomrath and Brogg and the others. He had begun to make his hop the day he secured the African retreat for himself. Now he was merely completing the logical course of action.

It was late afternoon by the time Quellen arrived. The sun was dipping to the horizon, and colors danced on the polluted lake. Lanoy was waiting for him.

"Everything's ready, Quellen," he said.

"Good. Can I rely on you to be honest?"

"You let me go, didn't you? There's honor even among slysters," said Lanoy. "You're sure you want to do this?"

"Positive. I can't stay here. I'm anathema to Kloofman now. I gave him an uncomfortable ten minutes, and he'll make me pay for it if he ever catches me. But he won't catch me. Thanks to you."

"Come inside," Lanoy said. "Damn you, I never thought I'd be helping you this way."

"If you're smart," said Quellen, "you'll go the same way. Kloofman's bound to catch you sooner or later. It can't be avoided."

"I'll take my chances, Quellen." Lanoy smiled. "When the time comes, I'll look Kloofman in the eye and see if I can't strike a deal with him. Come along. The machine's waiting."

sixteen

It was done.

There was a swirling and a twisting, and Quellen felt as if he had been turned inside out. He was floating on a purple cloud high above some indistinct terrain, and he was falling.

He dropped, heels over head, and landed in a scrambled heap on a long green carpet. He lay there for a moment or two, breathless, clutching at the carpet for stability in an uncertain world.

A handful of the carpet tore off in his hands. Quellen looked at it in puzzlement.

Grass.

Living grass. Strands of it in his clenched fingers.

The clean smell of the air hit him next, almost as a physical shock. It was painful to pull air like that down into his lungs. It was like inhaling in a room with full oxy turned on. But this was outdoors. The air in Africa was not like that, because it held an overstratum of residues from the more densely populated regions of the world.

Quellen gathered himself together and stood up. The grassy carpet extended in all directions, and in front of him there was a great thicket of trees. Quellen looked. A small gray bird came out on the overhanging branch of the nearest tree and began to chirp, unafraid, at Quellen.

He wondered how long Kloofman's minions would search for him before they concluded that he had hopped. Koll would be apoplectic. And would Kloofman cope with Lanoy? He hoped not; Kloofman was a sinister unreal monster, and Lanoy, despite his slyster habits, had a sense of honor.

Quellen began to move toward the forest. He would have to locate a likely stream and build some sort of house next to it, he decided. Improvised architecture—he'd make out, though his first attempts might not be very impressive. It would be *his* house, at any rate.

He felt no guilt at having taken this route. He had been a misfit, thrown into a world he could only hate and which could only ensnarl him. Norm Pomrath had taken this route. Brogg had. Now it was Quellen's turn. At least, before he had left, he had made a valiant try to defend himself against that world. It had been madness to think that he could match guile with the High Government. But he had shaken Kloofman, at least for a few minutes, and that was a worthy accomplishment. He had shown he was a man. Now valor's part dictated a quick exit, before Kloofman's superior might crushed him.

Two deer came bounding out of the forest. Quellen stood aghast. He had never seen land animals of that size, not even in Africa. The African mammals had long since been penned in preserves. Were these creatures dangerous? They looked gentle. They skipped off across the plain.

Quellen's heart began to throb as he filled his lungs with the sweet air. Marok, Koll, Spanner, Brogg. Kloofman. Helaine. Judith. They began to fade and blur. Social regurgitation. Quickboats. Good old Lanoy, he thought. He'd kept his word after all. Back to an unspoiled continent.

The world is mine, Quellen thought.

A tall redskinned man emerged from the forest and leaned against a tree, regarding Quellen gravely. He was dressed in a leather belt, a pair of sandals, and nothing else. The redskinned man studied Quellen for a moment and then raised his arm in a gesture Quellen could not fail to interpret. A warm feeling of comradeship glowed in Quellen. This man welcomed him. This man did not fear him.

Palm upraised, smiling at last, Quellen went forward to meet him.

AVON ◆ New Leader in Science Fiction